FLAWLESS REBELLION

LYNN HAMMOND

© 2019 Lynn Hammond
Print Edition

All rights reserved. No part of this book may be used or reproduced in any manner whatsoever without written permission, except in the case of brief quotations embodied in critical articles and reviews.

This book is a work of fiction. The names, characters, places, and incidents are products of the writer's imagination or have been used fictitiously and are not to be construed as real. Any resemblance to persons, living or dead, actual events, locale or organizations is entirely coincidental.

ACKNOWLEDGMENTS

I want to thank everyone who has read and corrected my paper. Each person has truly been very helpful.

I cannot express enough thanks to my editor, Monica Bogza of Trusted Accomplice. I was given her information from another author to help me on my new journey of becoming a writer. I am grateful for her friendship, advice, and late nights where we talk about my books. Thank you for your dedication and hard work.

To my family, who has supported me in this decision to start writing. I work a full-time job then come home and write until bedtime. My husband and kids have shown so much support; they even sit on the couch with me while I type.

To Bella Media Management for the cover for my book. I am amazed at the perfect result. Thank you, Darren Birks with Book Covers and More, and Darren Birks Photography, for the awesome photo of model Tiffany McNeil.

Thank you to my husband, who also took the time to read and pushed me to go after my dream.

To all my author friends who took time out of their work to help me with mine. You all welcomed me with open arms, and I am so thankful. Thanks, Authors Jordan Leger and Libby. J (Barnfield)

To all my readers who enjoy this book.

ALSO BY LYNN HAMMOND

In publication order
Alaskan Love Voyage
Alaskan Snowbound

Loving Lies Series
Risky Lies
Bloom

The Chaplain Series
Sacrifice for Love (Linkin's story)
Surrender for Love (Darcy's story)
Discovering Love Again (Malcom's story)

Dirty Secret Series
Lustful Money Book 1 (Tawney and Cole's story)
Stand My Ground Book 2
(Lindsay and Grover's story)

Other
Loveless Arrow
A Heart of Three

1

Emma

"EMMAAA!!" I shoot up in bed, clutching my chest when I hear Dad's angry, bellowing voice. My heart gallops nineteen miles to the dozen like a runaway horse finally given his head. I reach over and grab my phone to check the time. Shoot, it's eight-fifteen; I'm late for school.

After throwing on a red lace bodysuit and my favorite pair of black skinny jeans along with a pair of red suede ankle boots, I sprint to the bathroom for a look in the mirror and to apply my makeup. This outfit is so not approved by the school dress code, but I love to live rebelliously. Dad always makes a fuss about what I wear, how caked my makeup is, and he's always saying clowns wear less, but he doesn't understand how important my image is.

"Emma Leigh Sparks! Get your butt down here right now!" Uncle Linkin hollers this time instead of Dad.

Ugh! I better get down there, or both will be up here so fast and ground me till a month of Sundays. I really do think they both love being the boss of me.

As I stomp my feet on every step on the way down, I see my pipsqueak of a brother, Beckham, standing on the last one. He's holding onto my stash of e-cig fillers. He knows I'd be grounded for life if Dad or Linkin were to find out or get a hold of these.

"What do I have to do now, you little jerk, for you not to open your mouth and tell on me?" I ask while snatching them from his hand.

"I noticed you've got tickets to the Monster Jam this weekend. I think UJ and my buddy Chris would love to go to that." He crosses his muscular arms over his wide chest.

I'm the oldest, but Beckham is already six feet tall and looks like the Incredible Hulk. My brother thinks he can intimidate me, but he knows what I'm capable of.

"Too bad, baby brother. Iker is coming by to pick me up and take me to it. It's our six-month anniversary."

Iker and I met at a Turn Up the Heat party on Jessica's parents' one-hundred-acre property. Jessica is the popular girl at school, and if you are invited, you better show up. Somehow, that morning, an invitation ended up in my locker, so I told Dad I'll be studying with my friend Maranda, at her house.

I stop on the step above my brother and stand eye to eye with him. With my charming smile, I say, "If you are a good boy," I pat the top of his head, "I'll take you to the movies and buy you an ice cream after."

He pushes my hand away. "You're such a bitch, Emma. I bet if I tell Dad that you're sneaking out every night to meet up with Iker at the end of the street, he'd whoop your ass."

That little horse's ass likes to stick his nose into my business all the time. Before I can reply to the little shit, Dad approaches from around the corner.

"You are both grounded till I say otherwise. Now hand over your phones and get your asses into the car."

I'm so pissed now. My neck starts to burn, and the hair on my scalp starts to get tight. Sometimes I get so mad I just want to hurt someone or something.

"Really, Dad, I am not a little child anymore. You can't keep throwing my cellphone in my face every time I make a mistake."

I can't wait to move out on my own. This is my last year in high school, and I'm off to college right after. My GPA is 4.0, and I have a full ride to Clemson University. I can't wait for that either.

I love my dad, Uncle Linkin, Aunt Sophia, and Nova, don't get me wrong, but it will be great to get away. Nova came into my life when I was three years old, after my mom died. She really sits and listens to me. Aunt Sophia does too, but she's always so sad. I overheard her tell Nova that she wishes she could adopt another baby.

"Emma. Wait up." Nova comes running down the driveway after me.

I peek around her, and I catch a glimpse of Dad standing in the doorway.

"Emma, your dad is just being protective... and a douche," Nova says, handing me my cellphone. "The only reason you are getting it is because I asked him how he would get in touch with you if something happens." She winks.

Sweet.

"You're the best, Nova. Thank you." I turn around to head to my car.

"Oh, and, Emma!" Nova calls out. "Don't forget tonight is family night."

Ugh. Papaw and Grandma are coming over, and Sophia is cooking her famous meatloaf. Since my mom passed, her parents come over once a week to eat with us. They are pretty much up there in age. I don't ask them, and they don't tell. Dad tells me all the time how much I look like her, and it makes their day to see me. They love Beckham too, but he looks more like dad.

"I might be late. I have tutoring at four, but I will come home right after," I say quickly, worried she'll get mad too.

I finally get in the car. The clock on the dash says nine a.m. now. Great. Just great. I am super late now. Oh well, I will stay later today and do my assignment for English.

As I pull into Fort Mill High School, I see Iker talking to Maranda at the picnic tables. I wonder why they are not in class and why she is talking to my boyfriend. I take a deep breath. There is no way my best friend is messing with him. She is in love with Conner. Plus, she hates Iker and tells me all the time to dump his sorry ass.

As I step out of my car and hit the lock button, it makes a beeping sound that has the two of them turning toward the noise. They both watch me until I get closer.

"Where have you been? I have blown up your phone a zillion times!" Maranda asks with a hand pressed to her hip.

"Hey, baby." Iker walks over and plants a big kiss on my lips. I can smell the stench of marijuana on his breath.

I step back but give him a sexy smile. "Sorry, woke up late then argued with my little brother, which cause a bigger mess with Dad. But I am here now. What were you two talking about, and why aren't you two in class?"

I place my hand on my hip as well, waiting for an answer. They both look at each other then back at me. Alrighty, then. I don't have time for this shit. I've got to get to class or I will be really grounded.

I step aside then go around Iker. I don't look back as those two just scurry up behind me.

Maranda nudges my shoulder and whispers, "He has a big surprise for you, and I'm not allowed to tell. But this weekend, you need to tell your parents you are staying at my house. That's all I can tell ya."

Okay, I feel instantly better. The tension in my shoulders vanishes.

Iker comes up to my side and laces our fingers together. He leans in. "I sure missed our early make-out session this morning."

It feels good to hear that. Sometimes, I just feel so alone when I know I have so many friends and family surrounding me. I brush off the sadness and head to class.

2

Emma

YEP, I AM going to be grounded for life. Time has slipped away from me during my tutoring session. Several other students have walked in, needing my help with their English papers. My job is just to guide them in the right direction, more about the main point of their story, but I end up helping them write the whole thing. Hey, I like a little extra cash filling my pockets. That's how I buy my stash. No one knows other than Iker and Maranda.

When I pull up in the driveway, I notice the front door is open and the hall light shines through the glass. That means someone is waiting for me, and I am so up shit creek without a paddle. I park the car beside Nova's new Koenigsegg Agera RS—supposedly the fastest car in the world. Dad says when she gets mad, she likes to take it to a private lot and just gas it. I need something like that too for when I need to get something off my chest. I'm pretty sure that would freak Dad out, however.

Maybe I can talk Nova into giving me practice lessons.

Someone clears their throat. Shit. Uncle Linkin. There he stands, leaning on Nova's car. It's so dark that I didn't see him.

"Where have you been, kitten?" he asks, pushing himself off and walking towards me.

Before I answer, I cut the car engine off, grab my stuff, and get out. I look around for Dad.

"Emma, your dad is not out here. He had to take Beckham to the hospital."

I feel my heart drop into my belly. "Is he okay? What happened?" I drop all my things and run to Linkin.

I can tell he's been crying; I can see his red-rimmed eyes.

"He left with a couple of buddies earlier, saying they were heading to the football game, but a police officer called your dad about an hour ago to say Beckham had been shot."

Just hearing the word *shot* makes me start to tremble. I might hate my brother, but it's a sibling's hate.

Linkin pulls me in a big hug and kisses the top of

my head. I feel the wetness on his shirt from my crying.

"Look, let's get in and put your stuff away. Then on the way to the hospital, you can tell me why you were running late and also not answering your phone calls."

Dang, I cut my ringer off while in tutoring class and just jumped in the car to hurry home. I totally forgot to turn it back on.

LUCKILY, LINKIN IS not mad that I was tutoring others, but the look he gave me made it clear that I was better not be lying. For a chaplain, he can be intimidating with his bulky figure, but he has the biggest heart in the world.

Sometimes I hear him talking with other soldiers on the phone, listening to their problems late at night. His voice echoes through my wall as he counsels them on their feelings at the time and how it is okay to be frightened. I like how he wants them to get all their frustrations out instead of keeping them bottled up.

Like I have room to talk. I hold all my emotions in.

I lean forward and hit the FM radio button then scan the stations till country music comes on. I open the dashboard, looking for my stash of arrowhead candy, but there are only empty wrappers. Beckham! I scream in my head. I'm going to choke him when I know he is okay.

Linkin laughs. "That boy will never learn, will he?"

"He is going to get a knuckle sandwich once I know he is okay."

"You remind me so much of Darcy. She was full of spunk too and didn't put up with anyone's bullshit." He winks and turns into the hospital parking deck.

Even though I was three when Momma passed, I remember crying myself to sleep every night. Once, I even chased after a woman in the grocery store, hollering Mom's name. This lady pushing a grocery cart looked just like her. They say your mind can project someone else when you yearn for them.

The hospital parking lot is packed. We drive around the front of the building to the back, where the urgent care is. Dad texts Linkin once we have pulled in, saying the bullet is out and they are wrapping his foot up.

"Well, I'm glad Beckham is okay and the gunshot wound is a minor thing, but, boy, he is going to face restrictions till he is old enough to move out." I shudder just thinking about his punishment.

"Wait till your dad gets a hold of you too. He was furious when he could not get in touch with you. You are going to have to do better, Emma. You are going

FLAWLESS REBELLION

to be eighteen in a couple of months, and there is no more being treated like a child."

"Believe me, I know. I get reminded of that constantly," I say through gritted teeth.

"Don't get sassy with me. I just want you to be ready for this big world. When you go to college, it will be a big eye-opener and lots of responsibilities. Plus, I won't be there to always save you from destruction."

I take a deep breath to calm myself before I say something I don't mean. I close my eyes and whisper to my mom up above. *Momma, I miss you so much. I wish you were here to guide me in the right direction. I love my family and wouldn't trade them for anything in the world, but I need you.*

A gentle touch slides down the back of my hair, sending chill bumps down my arms. I know Momma is here even though I can't see her. She shows up when I really need her. Like now. *Love you, Momma.*

★ ★ ★

THE WAITING ROOM is packed with patients. Adults and children sit sickly in the blue hospital chairs, waiting to be seen. We make it to the front desk where a lady in scrubs sits, typing away on her computer.

"Good evening, sir, what are you here for?" she asks.

"My nephew is in one of your rooms back there, being sewed up from a gunshot wound. We are here to check on him." Linkin rocks back on his heels. "His name is Beckham Sparks."

His skin has lost all color. For a chaplain, he really hates coming to visit anyone in the hospital. But I don't blame him. This is where Momma died.

The lady clicks on her computer's keyword. "Yes, he is in the recovery room. I will unlock the door. When you enter, go straight till you get to the wraparound nurse station then take a left. Your nephew is in room two."

The hallway is quiet. Cream-colored curtains are drawn closed on both sides of us. All I hear are beeping noises and low voices. I reach over and place my hand into Linkin's. I have no reason to be scared. I know my brother is okay, but looking around to see all this equipment all over and people sitting on stretchers, moaning against the walls, has me terrified.

Two officers are standing outside the room, talking to dad. Dad looks directly at me then back to the men. I can see the disappointment in his eyes. I hate that I do this to him.

"Emma, go inside with your brother and keep an eye on him. He is already trying to take off the wrap the nurse placed on him. We will be in shortly after I talk to the officers." He gives my back a little push toward the room.

I turn to get smart with him, but decide not to when I see how red his ears are. I have noticed when he is mad, his ears and the top of his forehead get beet red. Nova says it's the meanness trying to get out.

When I pull the halfway curtain, Beckham is leaned over, picking at the brown ACE bandage.

"Stop it!" I walk straight over and slap his hand. "You are so hardheaded sometimes."

I plop down in the uncomfortable-looking brown chair beside the bed.

"Can you believe I shot myself in the foot? Brodie brought a gun and was showing it off under the bleachers. He said there were no bullets in it, so I wanted to hold it, just wondering what it felt like."

"How many times have Sophia, Linkin, and Dad given us the 'don't play with guns' talk? You knew better, Beckham. As for Brodie, I am going to kick his ass when I see him at school."

Beckham scoots over, twisting around and placing his feet on the floor. "Don't even think about it, sis. I will tell uncle Linkin and Dad about your little smoking habit."

I get up, walk over to put my face close to his, and in my sweetest tone, I say, "Go ahead and tell. If you do, I will let everyone at school know what you do with Sophia's baby oil and how you get down with Pilates videos."

Just thinking about walking in on him in the den late one night sends a shiver of disgust down my spine. He was on the floor, masturbating to the video. It made me want to take some Clorox and bleach my eyes out.

I expected him to try to choke me, but he just sat there, staring at me. Oh, the horror.

"Are you two ready to go?" Uncle Linkin says, peeking in.

"Sure! Where is Dad?" I ask, looking around for him after giving Beckham a last quick warning look.

"He is at the nurse station, getting the discharge papers. The officers finally left." Then he turns to Beckham. "Boy, you know better than to play with guns, and the next time, you might not be so lucky."

I watch as my brother's face falls. It's hard to look tough when Linkin sounds so worried and disappointed. I know they care about us. I go help my brother off the bed, and we exchange a look.

We follow Linkin out without a word. I do reach over and pinch my brother on the sensitive fatty part of his arm, making him grunt.

"That hurt!"

I love picking on him. I smile. Even though he aggravates me, I sure would miss him if something bad happened. I need to grow up and keep my eye on him until college.

3

Emma

THE NEXT DAY, I have to go help Dad and Uncle Linkin set up the homeless shelter at the church. School is closed today for Teacher Work Day. Fall snuck up on us early this year. I went to each of our neighbors' houses this morning, asking for old, worn winter clothes, shoes, or anything to take with me to the church.

"Emma, come on. We are late already," hollers Dad.

I touch up my makeup just in case I see Iker. He said he would stop by and help set up the cots. Maranda will be showing up as well so she can mention my spending the weekend with her. I'm not grounded, but my punishment is to be forced to take my brother everywhere with me from now on.

I skip down the stairs, holding on to the side rail.

The last time I did this without holding on, I slipped and hit the hardwood floor. My tailbone hurt for two months. I jump off the last step then walk over to put my boots on.

There are several male voices at the door. One sounds familiar, but I don't recognize him. After I finish zipping my shoes, I walk over and crack the door to get a glimpse.

A guy around my age stands with a large box in his hands, talking to Uncle Linkin. It is about forty degrees outside, and this dude has blue basketball shorts and a hoodie on. When he looks over at me, I notice his eyes are dark brown like a dark chocolate candy bar and his hair is dark brown too.

"Whoa, there, Emma." Dad holds his hand out, stopping me from falling on my face.

I'm so embarrassed. I missed all the steps while walking down the porch from eyeing the new guy. I can feel my cheeks burn from humiliation.

"You okay?"

"Yes, I'm fine. I was doing a checklist in my head while walking, to make sure I have everything for the church."

Dad lets go of my shoulder and wraps his arm around me, kissing the top of my head. *Oh, Lord, just shoot me now. How embarrassing, your father kissing you in front of a good-looking boy.*

The guy places the box down and walks over to me, holding out his hand. "My name is Az. I just moved here from the Philippines. My mother married an American man, and his business wouldn't let him relocate."

"Wow, welcome to Raleigh. You will love it here."

When we pull into the church parking lot, men, women, and children are lined up at the family life center. Maranda is already here, handing out the little bags we made up last Sunday. We put crackers, water, peanut butter, and a plastic knife in each pack. The homeless travel during the day to other places, but some work.

With all the stuff cleared from the trunk, I make my way into the kitchen to heat up the soups Sophia prepped up. I pour the potato soup into the large silver pot then turn the burner to medium heat.

A few minutes later, the kitchen is smelling wonderful from all the soups. I haven't eaten today, so my stomach grumbles, reminding me it's ready to be fed.

"Need any help?" Maranda walks in with empty pitchers. "Everyone loved Sophia's homemade lemonade-peach tea."

I walk over to the double fridge to grab the other drinks and turn to hand them to Maranda. "Hey, did you ask Dad about me staying with you this weekend?"

The look she gives me tells me that he said no. Ugh!

She starts to smile. "Just kidding. He said yes if you get all the chores done in the house, and Beckham's too."

"Seriously? This is not fair. I hate cutting the grass."

"Girl, you know I will help you. I need some exercise anyway on these wide hips. Pushing the lawn mower will help with that. Right?" She looks at me like I would know that.

Sometimes, she says the silliest stuff.

"Come on, you crazy girl. Let's get the soups out and refill their drinks. We will google how to use the push mower. I don't want you cutting off a foot or anything when you do try it."

Two hours later, the tables are wiped clean and all the trash put outside in the dumpster. I place the last of the dishes up in the cupboards.

Dad comes in with all the unused plastic utensils. "Thank you so much for helping out. Sophia is going to swing by on her way back from work to pick you up. Linkin and I have to get the guests sorted and ready for bed. Make sure Beckham takes his medication before going to sleep."

I can't wait until Nova gets back. I feel like the mom of the house, taking care of my brother when it should be either of them two.

Letting out a deep breath, I say, "Sure, I'll make sure he gets the poisonous apple before bed."

He just shakes his head and walks out. Hey, what can I say? I really love being the big sister.

After twenty minutes, I've laid out the cots for the women and children in the gym. Iker never called or showed up. I was really looking forward to seeing him. My phone vibrates in my back pocket, so I dig for it and glance at the screen. It's a tag from Jessica on Instagram.

That's weird. She never likes any of my posts or comments. Being suspicious, I click on the app and push below where she tagged me. A picture of her and Iker kissing each other on a bridge pops up. This can't be right. Why would he do this to me?

I hold my chest. I can't breathe. I must sit down. I walk over to the closet that holds our cleaning supplies, open the door, and walk in, shutting the door behind me. It's pitch dark in here. I flip over the mop bucket and take a seat. I put my elbows on my thighs, placing my face in my hands, and cry. I can't hold it any longer as my body starts to shake.

For the first time, my own anger lid bursts, and my face heats up. I come to my feet, standing there and debating what I need to do. I kick over a bleach tub in frustration, and that feels so good that I reach up to the shelf and use my arm to push all the cleaners onto the floor. The chemicals are burning my nose, but I don't care about the pain; it helps calm me down. I really need a smoke.

Still in shock, I step out of the messy closet, liquids have run under the door and cover a good distance of the floor. I peer up at Maranda standing there with her hand on the mop.

"What happened? Are you okay?" she asks, looking puzzled.

I try to speak, but nothing comes out, so I just nod.

Maranda starts walking towards me with a frown. "You saw, didn't you?"

The thought of what I just saw sends a sharp pain to my chest. I straighten up my shoulders, standing proud even though all I want to do is cry.

"How could I not? The bitch tagged me in the photo. I trusted him. I thought he really cared about me, but all I was to him was a name on his bedpost. Well, guess what? That will never happen. Oh, and when we get back to school, Jessica's going to wish she never messed with me." A sob catches in my throat.

Maranda wraps her arms around me, and I just let it go. I just want to be loved. I have this hollowed place inside that needs to be filled. I love my family and friends, but something else is missing.

4

Emma

Friday morning

I FEEL WARM wetness between my legs. Shit, not now... I need to decide if I sit at my desk until it's time to go or just get up and walk out now. My boyfriend cheats on me, and now this? I give up!

Groaning, I stand up and place my jacket around my hips. "Mr. Idlehorn, I have to go use the bathroom. I'll be right back."

"Emma, you have used up all your hall passes this year. Sit down. The bell will ring in ten minutes."

Okay, think, Emma. If I wait till then, the restroom will be jammed, but if I get up, then I will get detention. I bend down and unzip my bookbag. I take my cellphone out and text the only person I know who would do something completely stupid.

I throw my phone back in my bag then sit and turn

my attention back to the chalkboard where Mr. Idlehorn is writing our homework down.

The loud ringing of the fire alarm starts. The teacher is telling us to follow him. Guys and girls are pushing their chairs back and running toward the door. I get up, pulling down the jacket to make sure it covers my backside in case you can see the blood.

The halls are crowded with students running to the exit door. I run towards the bathroom to change my clothing.

"Emma, you owe me big time for this." Maranda's voice echoes in the bathroom.

"That's what besties are for." I flush the toilet and walk out to wash my hands.

"Come on, let's get out of here. Your annoying brother is outside, waiting for us."

Dang, I forgot all about him riding with me, but that is one of my chores now.

Opening the double metal doors, I glance around the crowded parking lot. Everyone is standing with their groups, talking while teachers walk around, doing a head count.

"All right, everyone. It's safe to get your bookbags and leave for the day. False alarm," Principal Holler says through the megaphone.

My phone vibrates.

Beckham: *Where the hell are you? My damn foot is killing me.*

Me: *Be there in a moment, jackass. Oh, and the door is unlocked.*

I start pushing my way through the crowd when I see Az talking to Beckham through the window of my car. When he follows Beckham's pointed finger, he is looking dead at me. I start to blush. Az is one sexy guy. I don't really ogle guys, but he just sends chill bumps all over my body when I'm thinking about what it would feel like to have his large, plumped lips touch mine.

A snap in front of my face has me blinking out of my daydream.

"You have it bad." Maranda laughs.

"Whatever. I just got my heart ripped out by Iker. I sure don't need to think about another guy right now."

I make my way over to the guys to see what is going on, but Iker steps in front of Az and me.

"Hey, sexy. You ready for this weekend? Pack some sexy clothes, bathing suit, and some booze." Iker leans down and tries to kiss me on the lips, but I push at his chest. He stumbles back but catches himself before he falls.

Az steps up in between Iker and I. "Emma, come

on. We've got to get going. Mom called. She needs me home to watch my little sister."

"Emma, we need to talk. That picture Jessica posted was fake. I would never cheat on you."

"I know it was you, Iker. Just go. We are through." I turn and head towards the car.

"Fine. You were just a piece of ass anyway. I have tons of girls waiting in line to go out with me." He flips me off.

I glance at Beckham, open my door, and hop in quickly. He knows being given the bird just pisses me off. "Az, hop in now if you need a ride," I holler out the window.

Az nods, sliding into the back seat. I crank the car, hit the reverse, and slam on the gas. I can see Iker in the rearview mirror. His eyes look like saucers. I swerve a little, missing him by inches.

"Stupid slut," he says, standing up from where he fell in the dirt. "You will pay for this."

"Stop the car, Emma," Beckham says. "I'm going to whoop his ass." He has his hand on the door handle, trying to open it.

"You are not going to do anything. I can handle my problems myself." I spin the tires out of the parking lot, burning rubber. "Okay, guys, Sonic sounds good right now, and it's half price till five on slushies. Let's go celebrate I didn't run over the asshole just now." I click the radio on, turning on some country music.

I'm glad nothing else was said during our drive. Listening to music calms my nerves but not these painful cramps below. I don't know why Eve had to eat the fruit off the tree. Now all women suffer from these God-awful periods, but on the bright side, chocolate always fixes it.

Az nods. "Sure, that sounds good. I will grab one for Ruby Lyn!" he hollers over the music.

I give him a thumbs up.

5

Az

THIS GIRL IS crazy with a capital C. I wasn't sure if I should get in the car, but Beckham begged me to get in. Plus, when my mother called, saying she needed me home right away, the offer sounded good.

The whole school has been talking about Emma and that guy, Iker, all morning long. If I didn't already have something on my record from fighting, I would have hit him right on the base of his nose, bringing him down to his knees. I was taught to treat girls with respect, no matter the consequences.

"Dude, look who is here." Beckham points to the pink Eclipse parked a few spots away.

Amanda and some of her friends are sitting on the hood of her car, talking. I finally agreed to go on a date with her over text. She's been trying to get me to say yes for days. She is a super nice chick and sexy as hell, but I really don't want to settle down since college is next fall.

Now, Emma, I wouldn't even blink an eye if I had a chance with her. We are both going to the same college. I got a full ride to Clemson on several scholarships I won by entering a writing contest. And I got a little scholarship money to help with books from Christian foundations where I did some volunteer work back home and in the states.

"Earth to Az." Emma snaps her fingers, bringing me out of my thoughts. "It's your turn to order. What do you want to get?"

I scoot up, ducking my head in between Emma's seat and the window to make my order. She turns, looking at me sideways, and her lips brush the side of my face. Time freezes for a moment.

"Oh my God, I'm so sorry. I didn't mean to kiss you. Shit! I was going to ask you not to forget your sister's order. I'm so embarrassed."

I smile at her nervousness. "If you wanted a kiss, why didn't you just say so?" I wink at her.

Her cheeks turn red. "I'm joking with you, Emma. Yes, get Ruby Lyn a grape slushy with nerds."

The waitress rolls in on skates and delivers our drinks to Emma. The girl leans down, hovering over the window. "Who is Az?" she asks.

"Um, me. Why?"

"Oh, that girl over there," she points to where Amanda is looking over and waving once our eyes meet, "she says not to forget about your date tonight." Then the waitress grabs the ice cream sundae that was still on her tray and hands it to me through the window. "She bought you a dessert. She wants to make sure you are sweet for tonight."

I take the ice cream, unsure what else to do. "Okay, thanks." I wave to Amanda. "Emma, let's go before she starts to walk over here."

"Wow! I'm impressed, man. Usually, the guy has to fork out the goods, but this chick is generous. Ask her tonight if any of her friends are single."

Emma's hand comes off the steering wheel and whacks Beckham on the back of the head. "Hell, no, you won't. I can't stand none of those girls over there. No way."

Damn, that hit was hard. He rubs the back of his head and punches her in the arm. They both start cussing at one another.

"Hey, guys? Can you finish your childish fight when you get home? You are making a scene." And I want to be out of here.

Half of our school is sitting in their cars at the drive-through. Everyone is watching us and laughing.

Emma jerks the gear to reverse, hitting the gas hard. The tires squeal loudly, and the smell of burnt rubber floods my senses. Something is really going on in her mind. I asked Beckham what her deal is with the attitude earlier, but he said it was just her being a typical female. The first time I saw her, there was a sadness about her.

She wouldn't make full eye contact with me. She would just look over my shoulder. I'm the type of person who wants to cheer everyone up, but Emma, she is holding onto something dark, and I'm not sure if I can help.

Relief sets in when we finally pull into my driveway. Racking my brain to try to figure Emma out is making me stir-crazy. Maybe this date with Amanda would help.

Ruby Lyn runs outside, holding Bo in her arms. This dog is a demon. It's a Boston terrier but looks like a damn catfish. His eyes poke out so far it looks like they'll both just fall to the ground at any moment.

"What the hell is that, man?" Beckham asks, pointing at Bo.

I laugh. "It might be little, but it is mean as hell. His teeth are razor sharp." I hold up my right ankle and rest it against the front seat. "See those scars? That was from him."

"Damn. I'm not getting out." He shakes his head.

Emma opens the car door and pushes the seat up so I can get out. She walks over to my sister then leans down to Bo. "Hey, buddy. Aww, you're such a cutie. Yes, you are," she baby-talks to him. His little nub of a tail just wags.

She stands up, smiling. "And you, pretty girl, must be Ruby Lyn. I'm Emma." They both giggle when Bo licks Emma's face.

"All right, time to go in. Mom said she prepped dinner and it's in the fridge, so we need to go in and get things started." I motion with my hand for my sister to run inside. Ruby skips away, waving before heading back in.

"She is adorable. Anytime you two want to come over, you're more than welcome." Emma smiles.

That gets my attention. Maybe I can spend time over there, be friends first, and work on getting her to talk to me. I wink at her. "That's a deal."

6

Emma

I TOSS AND turn all night long. Az and Ruby Lyn are coming over to stay the night since his parents had to fly back to the Philippines for a family emergency. After texting back and forth all weekend, all I have been doing is thinking about him. There is something different about him than the other boys at school. He is very cultivated.

He is so hot. I would love to comb my fingers through his thick ebony hair.

I roll out of bed then throw on a pair of pajama pants. I made sure to set my alarm for six-thirty a.m. I don't want to be late for school today. First thing on my agenda is finding Beckham's friend Brodie and giving him an earful.

I head down to the kitchen to make some breakfast and get my lunch. Sophia told me last night she made

Beckham and I club sandwiches. Just thinking about it makes my mouth water.

I walk past Beckham's room on the way and see Az sitting at the end of my brother's bed, looking through his bookbag. Why is he here now? He is supposed to stay tonight.

I grab my hair and twist it up into a bun on top of my head. My medium-length hair is all knotted from tossing and turning on the pillow last night.

Clearing my throat, I say, "Good morning, Az. You're here about eight hours early." I cross my arms to cover my breasts since I don't have a bra on. They are hard and poking through my tank top.

When he looks up, his eyebrows lift and his lips break into a big smile. "Aww, I've missed you and thought I would come on over now. Our friendship starts today."

"Okay, smart-ass. Just asking a question. Where is Ruby Lyn?" I'm not sure why I asked about his sister, but he just makes me nervous. I usually don't let anyone get to me.

"She's downstairs with Sophia and Nova, helping make breakfast."

"Okay, well, I'm heading down for some coffee and a pop tart. See you soon." I turn around and trip on one of Beckham's shoes lying out in the hallway. My knees are throbbing from the fall.

I can feel my cheeks get hot. I'm mortified. I start laughing to help with my embarrassment. I grab a hold of the door frame, using my other arm to push myself up.

"Lord, Emma, you okay?" Az asks, placing his strong hands under my arms to help me up.

I stumble, but balance myself enough before I fall forward. Az wraps his arms around my waist, pulling me against his chest. I freeze. My heart starts to beat so fast that it hurts. I want to turn around so badly and press my lips to his. But I'm afraid to get close. I've already been hurt.

He takes a step back, blowing out a breath. "Let me take a look." He squats down in front of me and looks at my knees. He brushes his fingers on my left one, and it automatically starts to burn.

"Ouch!" I wince.

I hear pounding footsteps coming up the stairs. Max comes to a halt at the top. A deep growl bubbles from his chest. The hairs on his back stand straight up, and his ears are pinned back as he lowers his front paws. He is about to attack Az. Our boxer is very scary and unpredictable with his moods.

Without turning around, I say, "Az, do not move. Max thinks you hurt me, and he is ready to attack. Be very still."

I move away from Az and walk straight towards

Max. His little tail nub starts to wag. "Hey, sweet boy. It's okay. I'm okay." I sweet-talk him until he finally sits down and lets me rub him.

"Time to eat, guys." Sophia's voice echoes from the bottom floor.

"Come on, boy, let's go get some food." I head down the stairs, my knees still burning like they are on fire.

I reach the kitchen with Max in tow. Dad is sitting at the table with his iPad blasting about the weather. I told him he should have just been a meteorologist.

I plop down in the chair beside him and snatch up a piece of bacon, placing it in my mouth.

"Emma, do I need to cut your fingers off? Go make your own plate. Oh, and where are your brother and Az?" He looks up from his tablet.

"Beckham was in the shower, and Az is about to head down. I fell in the hall, hurting myself, and Max thought Az hurt me. I had to make sure he didn't attack him."

At that exact moment, Max decides to growl, looking straight towards the kitchen entrance.

"Sit down, now!" Dad says. Max obeys but keeps his eye on Az.

"Come on in. He is bluffing. Just grab yourself a piece of bacon and feed it to him. He will be your best bud."

Az does what Dad says, and Max is now laying his chin on his leg, eating bacon. Traitor.

★ ★ ★

WE ARE ALL piled in the car, heading back to school. After I explained how Max acted, Uncle Linkin said he is very protective of women. He told us that Max growls at him sometimes when he chases Sophia around the house.

"Aren't you a little curious why Linkin would chase Sophia around the house?" Beckham says with a laugh. "I think he was trying to cop a feel."

I just shake my head and giggle. That is something I do not want to think about. I cringe.

Everyone has sex. That's part of life, but just thinking about my family having sex makes me shiver.

"Are you cold?" Beckham reaches over and turns the heat on.

It's fall, so I can blame it on that. "Just a little. Got an abrupt chill out of nowhere." The roar of hot air comes out of the vents. I look in the rearview mirror, and Az winks.

I wink back. A little flirting is not going to hurt anything. I look back straight ahead and make sure I keep my attention in front of me.

"Well, shit! Dumb ass is parked beside us," Beckham says.

When I turn to look out the passenger side window, I see Iker is stopped at the light and Jessica is sitting in the center, right beside him. That bitch always likes to have someone's seconds. For someone so rich, you'd think she could snag a good guy, but money can't even buy her crazy ass a boyfriend.

7

Emma

It's fifteen minutes before the bell rings. Today has been a hell of a day. Iker keeps blowing on the back of my neck in class. I'm really trying to ignore him. I really am, but my body is betraying me. What can I say? I like bad boys. I'm aware that he is a player and I'm going to get hurt, but I really want to go to the Monster Jam and see how things go.

I turn around. "You have five minutes to tell me what the hell is going on between you and Jessica. I'm not one of those girls who just fawn over you. I have goals, Iker. I really want to go hang out with you this weekend, but I won't if you are hung up on Jessica. You can't have us both."

He leans in close, our lips almost touching. Mrs. Abernathy's voice fades out from the chalkboard. "I'm sorry. Jessica took that picture right before I pushed her off. She's friends with my oldest sister. She's constantly nagging me to go out with her, but I keep telling her no. You've got to trust me."

I blow out a breath. "Okay, but why was she in the middle of your seat today on the way to school?"

"She scooted over before I could tell her no. When I saw your car pull up beside me, I knew why she did it." His hand comes up to brush away some of my loose hair that fell in my face. He places it behind my ear then runs his finger down my neck and around to my chest. Chill bumps spread down my whole body. "Just trust me. That's all I ask." His hand disappears, and I miss the touch right away.

Don't do this, Emma. He is not good for you.

I sigh. "Okay, I believe you. I'll text you later."

Please let me be making the right choice.

Iker's lips touch mine softly before he pulls away. He gives me a wink and falls back into his seat. I just shake my head but smile too. I think everything will be okay.

The bell rings overhead. I can smell cologne and marijuana beside me. I know it's Iker. He bends down and grabs my bookbag from beside me. "I'll carry this for you." He smiles.

"Well, thank you, sexy." I scoot out of my seat and follow him out of the classroom.

He reaches down and intertwines his fingers with

mine. All the kids look down to our joined hands. Some of the girls are looking at me like they want to come straight over and gouge my eyes out and pull my hair out by the roots.

"Don't mind them. They know who I want. They're just jealous," Iker mumbles in my ear.

I turn my head and look up. He winks. I smile, but deep down, I know this is too good to be true. Anything in my life that could possibly make me happy always blows up in my face.

Someone bumps my shoulder, and I lose my balance. I fall backwards, my hand slipping out of Iker's, and I hit the floor hard, right on my ass. A sharp pain shoots from my tailbone and down my left leg.

"Oh my God," I holler out loud.

"I'm so sorry, Emma. Are you okay? I didn't see you," Jessica says with a sly, knowing smile on her face.

"You bitch." I remember some of the wrestling moves Beckham showed me.

I grab her ankle, pulling it hard towards me. She tumbles back, falling straight on the hard tile floor. I situate myself on my knees. The pounding pain from my tailbone makes me grunt. I get on top of her, pinning her arms with my inner thighs. I use all the strength I can muster to hold them.

She starts bucking me, but I tighten my hold on her

body. Crowds of students are surrounding us. Iker is telling me to get off her before I get suspended. I don't care what happens. This whore is going to pay.

"Emma, stop it! She's not worth it." He pulls my arm, trying to pull me off her.

I jerk my arm away from his. I ball up my right hand into a fist, draw back, and slam it into the side of her face. She hollers. I do it again, but harder this time. She starts kicking her legs, and her knees are hitting me in the back. I don't feel any pain now, just relief.

I contemplate if I should hit her one more time before I get off her. My mind is telling me yes. I'm going to get in serious trouble, but the nagging feeling that pinches my chest tells me to make her suffer.

Remind her who she is messing with. She will never do this to you again, this little voice keeps telling me.

I grab the hair on both sides of her head with my hands. I roll it around my hands, tightening it, and I bounce her head up and down. I can hear the thumping as the back of her head hits the ground. Her body gets still.

Did I just kill her? I release her hair and look down. Her eyes are closed, and her face is bloody from the hit.

"What on God's green earth is going on here?

Emma, get off Jessica right this instant," Principal Green says through clenched teeth.

Crap! I'm in big trouble.

"Follow me, you two. Oh, and, Iker, you can come as well. I can tell this probably has something to do with you." The principal turns, heading towards the front office.

AFTER ONE HOUR of lecturing us and telling us how fighting doesn't accomplish anything, we both had to shake hands. I refused to touch the whore, but Mr. Green called my dad, and after being chewed out by him too and being grounded again, I shook the bitch's hand.

When I'm handed my slip for ISS for two days, I turn and walk out of the room without a word. Iker's parents didn't show up. They told the principal they were too busy to come. He said he would wait for me outside.

I head down Hall B toward the exit. I round the corner when I see Az. He is leaning against the brick wall with a confused look on his face. I don't understand why he is waiting on me. I thought he caught a ride with Beckham and one of their friends. And where is Iker?

"Have you seen Iker?" I ask Az as I get closer.

"I can't believe you got back with that douche," he

says, throwing his hands up in the air. "You know he is a player, right?"

"Look, he explained what happened. Jessica was the one who started all this drama. Why didn't you ride home with the guys?" I ask as if it's any of my business.

"I have Ruby Lyn after school, remember? So, anyway, I was at the car, waiting for you, when two girls came out. I overheard them talking about a catfight in Hall C. They said your name, so I ran back in, just at the time the principal got there."

I feel horrible, knowing Az is upset with me. I was really looking forward to us getting to know one another and to the fun games we are all going to play tonight. I just think we should be friends right now. I am not over Iker, and a relationship wouldn't be wise, although it seems he didn't wait for me as promised.

8

Az

WHEN I EXIT class, I immediately look for Emma. Beckham walks toward me with Brodie. "Hey, man." He nods. "We are heading to Adventure Air Sports to try out the largest trampolines in the world. You want to come with us?"

Dang, out of all the days to watch Ruby Lyn. "Man, I wish I could, but I got to take care of my little sister. Parents have already left, so I can't get out of it even if I wanted to."

"Crap, I forgot about that. I'll see you at home in about two hours, then. Maybe this weekend we all can go and have some fun together."

"Sounds good," I say.

I stand against the wall near the exit door, waiting for Emma. About ten minutes go by, and nothing. I head outside, thinking maybe she beat me out there. I walk over to the car, but she is not in it. I hear a loud shriek from one of the female students walking across the parking lot.

I wait a few more minutes till the two girls get closer. They're both talking loudly about a fight that's happened. I don't like to get into any drama, but my gut feeling is telling me Emma is involved somehow.

I head towards them, stopping right in front of them. "Hey, beautiful." I look at the one who's been running her mouth the whole time they were getting closer. "What's going on in there?" I gesture toward the school.

"Jessica bumped into Emma. She saw her holding hands with Iker and got pissed. She pushed her to the ground." She starts twirling her hair and popping her gum.

"Well, thanks, babe. I guess I better get back in there to make sure Emma is okay."

I brush past them, leaving the two standing there.

"Oh, you don't have to worry about Emma," the girl calls back over her shoulder. "She's the one pounding the crap out of Jessica."

Well, shit. I start running back to the school. Emma finds trouble wherever she goes. I can't believe she got back with that lowlife piece of cheating shit. I swing around the corner where students are crowded, and I see Emma on top of Jessica, and Principal Green hovering over the two of them.

I slip farther down the hall, bumping people as I go. From a distance, I see Iker standing beside Emma with his hand on the middle of her back. They head down the hall toward the office.

"Hey, Az." Amanda pops up in front of me with her eyes wide. "Why have you been ignoring me?"

Shit. I have been avoiding her. I was hoping I'd be staying over at Emma's house tonight and we would get to know one another better. I was going to ask her to a movie.

"Hey, Amanda. Sorry. I have been a little busy, watching my sister after school, and now my parents are out of town. I'm staying with Beckham and his family."

I feel like shit for lying to her, but I am telling her half of the truth at least.

"Oh, okay. Well, I got to go too. I have track practice." She turns around, but not quickly enough, and I see her frown.

Dammit to hell. I don't want to lead her on, but Emma is back with Iker, so why not just date? "After practice, do you want to come over to Beckham's tonight to play a couple games and eat pizza?"

Please say no. Please say no.

"I'll be there," she says cheerfully.

Damn.

Well, tonight will be very interesting for sure. What did I just do? I make my way down the hall to wait on Emma. I feel the buzz of my phone in my pocket. I take it out and take a look. It's a text that has come through.

Beckham: *Bro, you still at school?*

Me: *Yes. Emma got into a fight. She is in the principal's office.*

Beckham: *Dad just called me. He is pissed. On my way home now. I'll watch Ruby Lyn till you get there. Oh, and watch out. Emma got ISS, so she is going to be a nightmare to deal with all the way home.*

I lean against the wall again, waiting on Emma. Iker walks by with this big shit-eating grin on his face. He makes me want to pound him into the ground.

"Hey, Az. Oh, guess what? Emma and I are back together. Stay the fuck away from her. You hear me?"

I narrow my eyes. "Well, that's going to be hard when I'm staying with her. I'll make sure I stay very close to her at game night tonight."

He is about to say something, but a teacher walks around the corner just at that moment. Iker gives me an evil look and storms to the nearest exit.

★ ★ ★

"PEOPLE PUT THESE pink things in their yard and at the

beach," Amanda says, holding the card in her hand.

"Flamingos," Beckham blurts out.

"You are correct." Amanda places the card down.

We have been playing Taboo for nearly thirty minutes now. Our team is winning, of course. Emma and Amanda are on one team, and Beckham and I are on the other.

When Amanda knocked on the door, holding a six-pack of soda and dessert, Emma slammed the door shut right in her face. She hollered for me to come over.

"Really, Az? You invited your little girlfriend over here? I think I have had enough shit for one day, don't you? I really can't take any of her whiny talk tonight." Emma turned briskly, bumping me hard with her shoulder as she walked past me.

I just shook my head at her in disbelief. I welcomed Amanda in, and for now, Emma has been playing nice. She seems to be having a good time.

Amanda's high squeal brings my attention back to the table. Emma is talking about getting hot and bothered. I am stunned for a second. Beckham pushes the buzzer. It rings loudly.

"No more, sis. I don't want to hear that kind of talk from you. It's not sexy at all." He puts it up to her ear, buzzing it again.

She slaps it out of his hand. "You ass. How about

dampened?"

That got my attention. "Wet!"

"You got it right." She wiggles her finger at me. "You dirty dog. I bet you get all those girls wet with those big brown eyes of yours." She slaps her hand over her mouth, laughing.

She stumbles back, falling onto the couch. I walk over to take a seat beside her and whisper, "Are you high?"

"Just a little." She does the hand gesture for it, then she crashes her lips to mine.

I moan into her mouth when she deepens the kiss. Her arms wrap around my neck, pulling me closer. Her tongue slips to the edge of my lips. I can taste a little mint mixed in with menthol.

A hard slap pushes my forehead to hit against Emma's. "Get your tongue out of my sister's mouth, man. Not cool at all."

We both pull apart, breathless. Emma stands up abruptly. "Oh my God! I am so sorry. I'm really fried." She runs out of the room, and her feet stomp against the stairs.

"I know now why you have been avoiding me. You have a thing for Emma," Amanda says. She storms off in the other direction, heading towards the front door.

Damn. I run after her. I reach her before the door

can close. I grab her arm, swinging her body around to face me. "Look, my life is complicated right now. I should be living a teenage life, but I'm usually the one taking care of my little sister. Yes, I have a thing for Emma. The first time I met her, something drew me to her."

"You could have just been honest. I can tell you now, Emma is hooked on Iker. When he gets his sight on someone, he doesn't let them go without a fight. But once he loses interest, then you're good to go. I would know. He did that to me after he got what he wanted." A few tears drop from her eyes.

I reach out, pulling her to me and wrapping my arms around her. Her shoulders begin to shake. She deserves better. I can't be the one for her, but I want her to know that I'm not an asshole.

After a few minutes, she steps back. She looks up at me, eyes all puffy, and mascara lines running down her face. Her lips tremble. "I'm sorry." She wipes her eyes free of tears.

"No, I'm the jerk. I'm sorry, but I hope we can be friends. I don't have a lot of them."

"Sure. But once Emma breaks your heart, I'll be waiting to pick those pieces up." She winks then turns to walk down the path to her car.

Alrighty, then.

9

Emma

I CAN'T BELIEVE I was so stupid. I kissed Az. During the question, he hollered out "wet" for the answer. I got wet myself. His voice sent chills down my body. When I looked at him, I saw the intense stare he was giving me. He wants me.

I look out my window, watching Az and Amanda hug. I don't understand why it should bother me since I'm back with Iker, but it does. I walk back over to my bed, flopping down on my stomach, and dial his number.

The weak moment I had with Az needs to be erased. Sneaking out for a little bit will do me some good. I hid the emergency hang ladder under a box of mom's stuff in the closet. Once I know everyone is nestled in bed, I'll make my escape.

I'm lying down on the bed, watching Netflix on

my computer, when someone knocks on my door. I wonder who that could be.

"Come in," I say, rolling over to my side then scooting up into a sitting position.

Az walks in, shirtless. He pulls up his drawstring camouflage pajamas that rest a little below his hips. I notice he has a dark happy trail below his belly button running down under his pants. I think that's the sexiest thing I have ever seen. I just want to reach over and trace it with my fingertips.

"Hey," I say a little shyly. I look into those powerful, sexy brown eyes. I have just been caught checking him out.

He clears his throat. "Can we talk?"

"Sure," I reply.

Az walks over to the bed and sits down on the opposite side of where I sit. Well, that sucks. I mean I need to keep my distance, but him sitting that far from me kind of hurts.

"I like you, Emma. In my country, men treat their women like queens. We are just teenagers, and we should be having the time of our life, but you have captured my heart." He shifts closer to me.

I have captured his heart? We only kissed. I grab my pillow, wrapping my arms around it, afraid I might touch him.

"Since the first day I met you, I've had this electric

pull towards you. I dreamed about you before I met you. It sounds weird, right?"

I have no idea what to say. I place my palm on the side of his face then slowly slide it down. I cup the back of his neck, pulling him towards me. He watches me with those sinful brown eyes for a moment. No words, no smile.

I lean over so my mouth is an inch from his and whisper, "I feel it too." I place a soft kiss against his lips. "But I have promised to give Iker another chance."

"Wow. Okay, if that is your decision. Friends is what we will be." He gets up and walks out of my room, not looking back at me.

I watch him leave, wondering if I've made the right decision.

I WAKE TO a tapping on my window. Shit, I must have cried myself to sleep, thinking about my mom, wishing she were here with me. I don't remember her much, but the stories Dad and Uncle Linkin tell me help to have her close. They tell me I am just like her. Hard-headed, they say. I smile, thinking about that.

Another thump sounds from the glass. I scoot out of bed and head to see what that noise is. I grab the string, pulling it down to pull up the blind. I look down. Iker is standing below. He winks.

I slide up the glass slowly and quietly. Everyone is probably asleep, but I can't take any chance that one of them might be coming in, especially Dad. He is way overprotective of me. He says, "Baby girl, that's what dads do. We protect our princesses."

Next week, I will be eighteen. An adult. Will my father still call me a princess then?

"You ready to go, babe?" Iker quietly calls from below.

"Be right down." I head quickly to the closet and throw the items off the hidden ladder.

I make sure the strong steel hooks are attached to the wood window frame before I extend it over the window, letting it hang on the outside. I lift my left foot over the frame and place it on the step. I steadily rise, using my arms as I balance myself to get over to the outside window. Both of my feet are planted on the metal rung, and I take a moment to listen for any sounds. I take a couple steps down, making sure to hold on tightly to the window. I look down, and I suddenly start to feel woozy. I close my eyes and count to ten. My legs start to get wobbly. Shit...

"I got you, baby," Dad whispers in my ear.

At that moment, I'm glad to hear his voice.

"I can't move. I'm afraid I will fall."

"Malcom, I got the extension ladder. I'm coming up," I hear Uncle Linkin's voice from below.

These two amaze me with how much they love me and get along. Sometimes, I hear Linkin slip up and call me his girl, but he brushes it off when I ask him about it. Dad just says since he and Sophia can't have children, they think of us as theirs. My dad encircles his arms around me but places both hands on each side of the ladder.

"Okay, baby girl. Your dad is going to step over to my ladder while I stand down below. We are not going to let anything happen to you. You understand?" Uncle Linkin says softly.

I shake my head. My face is still plastered against the cool steel step above me. I try to speak, but no words come out. I feel like there are a ton of bricks on my chest, and my lips are tingling, and my mouth is bone dry.

I feel Dad shift, and his strong hand grips around my waist. He pulls me against his chest. I keep my eyes closed, scared to look down.

"Emma, I'm going to lift you, and we are moving to the next stand. Just be still."

We get over, and Dad gets us situated. "Okay, I'm going to take a step down, then you will do the same. I will be behind you the whole time."

"O-okay, Dad," I stutter.

I know one thing; I will never try to climb out of a window again. I don't care what happens. This is so terrifying. I hold on tightly to the steps of the ladder. We head down each one carefully. Dad's soothing words in my ear help, and I start feeling motivated.

"That's my girl. A few more steps, and we will be on the ground," Dad says.

I'm swept up into my dad's arms immediately when we get to the ground. He cradles me just like when I was a baby. I turn into his chest while he rocks me, and I cry. My whole body just shakes so hard I think he will drop me. I tighten my hold around his neck. Snot is pouring out of my nose, and I turn my head right then left, wiping it on my dad.

His deep laugh makes me laugh. "Kiddo, please tell me you did not just blow your slime onto my shirt."

I giggle. My shoulders start to relax, and the numbness I was feeling in my legs starts to leave and my feeling comes back.

"Sweetheart, what were you thinking?" Aunt Sophia coos, rubbing my back.

I step back from Dad's arms and turn around. Everyone is standing on the lawn, including the neighbors. I scan the faces, looking for Iker's, but I don't see him. I let out a breath.

"Why would you do this, Emma? You know how dangerous that is. What do you have to say about your actions?" Nova walks up, hands on both hips.

I'm shocked. Nova never gets angry. "I was sneaking out to go hang out with some friends. I'm about to be eighteen years old, and all of you treat me like I am still a baby." I step away from Aunt Sophia's touch. "And, Nova, you're not my mother."

Nova's hand slaps me right across my face. I touch the stinging area. I spear her with a deadly look. "Don't ever touch me again. You better be glad my mother isn't alive, because she would whoop your ass."

"Emma Sparks, apologize right now," Dad says as Nova cries in his arms. Why do I hurt the ones I love? She's not my mother, but she has raised me as her own.

"I'm sorry. I don't know what is going on with me."

"We will discuss your attitude later. For now, back in the house, up to your room, and your phone will be staying with me."

"Yes, sir," I grumble, heading to the door. I notice everyone standing on the lawn, watching me with disappointment in their eyes.

"Wow, sis. You sure know how to make an uproar. Next time you want to sneak out, you might want to ask me to help." Beckham snickers.

"Walk away, Beckham. Don't have time for your snide comments."

For the next hours, I listen to Dad's lecture about sneaking out. He goes on about how men are dressing up like clowns in dark-tinted vans and snatching up young girls for sex trafficking. How a young girl was followed into a mall, and when she came out, a van drove up right when she was opening the door and a guy leaned out the sliding door and grabbed her arm. Luckily, a guy saw what was happening and got to the girl in time before they got her in the vehicle.

My stomach drops at hearing this story. I hear all kinds of stuff on the news, teachers talking at school and on the radio about young teens being abducted.

I finally hug my family, promising I would not do that again. I head up the stairs, passing Beckham's room. The room is dark. I noticed Az didn't come down to see what all the ruckus was about. He's probably mad at me, and I don't blame him one bit.

10

Emma

Happy Birthday to Me

FRIDAY EVENING ROLLED around; I'm busy dolling myself up for tonight's extravaganza. Nova talked Dad into letting me go to Wilmington, NC, to one of her friends' beach house for a night. Her and Aunt Sophia will be our chaperones.

"So, what are you all planning for my party tonight?" I ask, placing my make-up into my duffle bag.

"I'll tell you, but act surprised because Nova would be upset I let the secret out of the bag," Maranda says, holding out her pinky.

She cracks me up with the pinky swear. "I promise." I laugh.

"Okay, we're going to a new club called Seven Points. This place has laser lights shining all around, and they have dancers about five feet in the air with outfits that glow in the dark, doing exotic dancing in front of flashing firework billboards. She said people stand in line for hours, waiting to get in."

"Really? That sounds amazing. I can't wait to shake my booty all over the dance floor. She really does love me, doesn't she?"

"She really does. That was wrong, what you said to her that night. She told me she just wants to make you happy and give you everything she never had."

I've been feeling bad since right after those words left my mouth. I was just upset and lashing out. She came up to my room later that night and crawled in bed with me.

"*Hey, sweetie. I know I'm not your mom, but I sure love you like you're my own. Did you know your dad asked me if I wanted to try to have a baby?*" *she said, taking a strand of my hair and twirling it around her finger.*

I smiled and turned over. Her eyes were red and swollen. I knew she'd been crying. "Really? What happened?"

"*You stole my heart that day in your princess bouncy house. You told your dad you missed me and I should have this perfect gift. You thought the blow-up would bring me back to you. When I got in, you know what you did?*" *She giggled.*

There was no telling what I did. I was only three at

the time, but I probably did something funny. "No, what?" *I scooted over, closer to her, and stared up at her like a little girl.*

"You jumped in my lap and shoved your fingers in my mouth. You were wired up on candy. You were a mess, but my mess. I just felt that you and Beckham were all I needed in my life, and I was content with that."

That's when I knew she was my mom.

"Yeah, I apologized. I was a total bitch."

Maranda is eyeing me with her piercing icy blues. She knows how hard I try to be a good girl. I can't control the little bitch that sits on my shoulder, ready to lash out.

"Okay, my little princess best friend," she says, mocking Dad's words.

We both fall over on the bed, laughing.

I've decided to wear my short black halter-top dress. The back shows off a little of my skin. With this dress, you can't wear a bra, but I've used some flower nipple stickers to cover my tits. I love the silky fabric on my skin. Nova gave me her hot-pink stilettos. These are my favorite pair. I can't believe we wear the same size, but it's a plus for me since she has some cool shoes.

"Damn..." Nova barges in, looking me up and down. "You look hot, and your dad is going to kill me." She smirks at me.

My dad worships the ground she walks on. She knows he will bitch at her a little but then calm down. Aunt Sophia says she was the one who saved my dad from depression after mom died.

I believe it because she bends over backwards for Beckham and me. The horror stories kids at school tell about their stepparents make me thank the good Lord above for blessing me with her.

Plus, my mom comes and sees me sometimes, letting me know she is watching over me. Only Dad and Uncle Linkin know because they both get visited too.

"Okay, time to get going," Nova grabs my duffle bag and heads out the door.

★ ★ ★

AN HOUR LATER, Nova pulls in the parking deck across from Seven Points Club. The pounding bass of hip-hop music pours out the open door of the nightclub. Two large burly men stand as sentries on each side of the door, checking ID's.

"Dang, the music is so loud, and look at all those people wrapped around the building just waiting to get in." Aunt Sophia's eyes widen.

I snicker. She doesn't really do the club thing. Crowds worry her, but Uncle Linkin says it's because of her tragic accident. No one talks about it, though.

"Why don't we just head in. If it's too much for you, I'll have one of my friends come, get you, and take you to the beach house." Nova gives Sophia's hand a little squeeze.

We get into the door, bypassing all the people waiting in line. I look over, and all the girls are giving us the stink eye. I just smile and turn and walk in. The DJ sounds great and just happens to be playing *Girls like you* by Maroon 5, one of my favorites. The dance floor is packed tightly with guys and girls. Everyone's bodies are bumping and grinding all over each other. A few high platforms, about four feet from the ground and gated, have couples in each one of them, dancing dirty.

Suddenly, a hand covers my eyes. "Honey, that is too much for my sweet girl's eyes," Aunt Sophia says in my ear.

I push her hand away. "That is nothing compared to our school dances."

Her eyes widen in shock. She opens her mouth, but snaps it closed. She looks just like Mr. Bubbles, my goldfish. Nova leads us upstairs to the top floor. There is a wraparound booth that has Nova's name on it. Once we take our seats, a waitress immediately comes over to take our order.

When she returns, she hands us some wristbands. "These allow you to get two drinks from the bar. I know you are not of age, but the boss said it was okay." She snaps them on our wrist.

I look over at Nova, and she winks. "Two drinks can't hurt you. I did give the bartender only a certain list for you two to choose from. Your dad would tan my hide if he knew, so it's our little secret." She looks over to Aunt Sophia, making it clear it goes for her too.

"Oh, my lips are zipped. I will be watching them very closely to make sure they are okay. Uncle Linkin would probably call the SWAT team on us if he ever found out." She shakes her head back and forth.

We sip on cosmopolitans since all the other mixed drinks are too stout for our taste. The cute bartender, Alex, gave us some samples of the most popular drinks to try, but this one was the best by far.

"All right, let's slurp the last drop down and wiggle our asses on the dance floor." Maranda smiles at me.

I lift my glass, and she holds hers up too. "Happy Birthday!"

The sweet taste goes down, and I can't wait to get back for another. Maranda and I stand up, making our way to the dance floor. The place is jam-packed.

We lose ourselves into the crowd, finding a spot near the center. I spent the last two songs dancing dirty with Maranda. We have drawn a lot of attention on the dance floor. Several guys have surrounded us, bumping and grinding with us. My boobs are drenched in sweat, and my calves burn from all the sensual, bending dance moves we're doing.

If Dad were here, he probably would have covered me with a blanket and dragged me off the dance floor. I smile, thinking about him and his overprotectiveness.

Maranda points behind me, and I turn, following in her direction. There, on the dance floor, is Jessica and Iker, grinding against each other. I'm a little confused about why they are here when it's hours away from home. And why is he with her? I push my way through the crowd, elbowing a few people who don't want to move out of my way quickly enough.

I stand with my arms crossed, waiting for them to recognize me standing here. Jessica is the one who notices first. The sneer on her face gives away that she knew I was here. I bet she planned this all along. She can't stand for me to be happy.

Iker throws his arms out at her, I guess in frustration that she stopped dancing. When he looks over his shoulder, his eyes are big as saucers. I read his lips. "*Shit!*"

I rear back my fist and punch him straight in the nose. "Fuck!" he screams, covering his bloody nose with his hand.

"What the hell, Emma?" He storms past me, heading away from me.

"Oh, not so fast, buddy." I snatch the back of his shirt, yanking him back, and he stumbles backwards. "You know, Iker, you two deserve each other. Both of you are self-centered asswipes. Just one question, though. Why lead me on then show up here for my birthday? Was it just to hurt me?" I was so upset and on the verge of crying. And I don't cry.

I stand tall, piercing him with my brown eyes.

"I didn't know you were going to be here. Jessica talked me into coming here for the weekend. Her friend's parents have a condo down here." He shrugs his shoulders.

"Look, I really like you, but I wanted someone who was not under strict rules. You are not able to go as you please like Jessica can. It's our senior year. I want to enjoy it." He breaks eye contact and looks me up and down. "Now, if you want to prove me wrong, let's head out back, and I'll give you the best birthday present you'll ever have."

Is he freaking kidding me? I'm standing there in shock.

Iker grabs me, pulling me up against him. "What'd you say, baby?"

I can't believe what I'm hearing. I guess punching him in the nose didn't hurt him enough. Daddy always said to use this self-defense move only if I felt threatened. At this moment, I think his big fat ego needs to be shown I'm the one in control here.

I smile and wink, making him relax and think we are about to head outside to have a little fun. He backs up a little, wiggling his finger for me to follow him. At that moment, I move my hip forward, bending my knee and kicking my leg out, hitting him right in the groin.

"Fuuck!" Iker gasps, grabbing his precious jewels and dropping onto his knees on the dance floor. People are scattering away from us.

Jessica comes running over, hollering Iker's name. She gets down on the ground beside him, trying to comfort him. "You are crazy, Emma. I think you need to call the cops, Iker, and have her arrested for assault."

Iker shakes his head, "No! Let's just go."

"Are you serious? She injured you twice." She helps him off the floor. He swats her hands away.

"I'm fine. It's her birthday, and we ruined it. What we did was a shitty thing to do. Come on, I need to ice this baby." He has his manhood still covered with his hands.

Maranda must have read my mind as she sticks her foot out when they're walking off. Iker and Jessica both go tumbling down, sliding across the shiny black-

and-white-checker floor.

The music has stopped. Loud laughing from the crowd echoes through the quiet club. A couple of people help them up, and Iker pushes them away. He shakes his head and walks off toward the exit with Jessica following behind him. Those two deserve one another.

Not a second later, the DJ blast the music back on, and everyone goes back to dancing like nothing happened.

"Damn, that was hilarious. Remind me not to piss you off, Miss Balboa." Maranda laughs, linking our arms together and dragging me toward the bar. "Let's get our last drink on. We might even talk Nova into letting us have a lemon drop. Whoop! Whoop!"

11

Emma

"I WILL NEVER drink again." I sit in the back seat with sunglasses on to protect my eyes from the bright light from the sun that glares through in the window of the back of the car.

Nova wouldn't let us drink more at the club, but once we got back to the beach house, we played a game of Ping Pong. Instead of beer, she put water in the cups, but there were Jell-O shots to the side for us to eat.

"Sweetie, you better sober up and fix yourself, or your dad is going to skin my hide," Nova says from the front seat. "Here. Take these." She hands me some Tylenol and a Gatorade.

Aunt Sophia watches me from the driver's mirror. I guess she is waiting to see if I will take it. She said she didn't get a wink of sleep last night, because she was worried about our heavy drinking. Nova told her it wasn't a big deal, because she knew when to stop with the shots. Even though I had only seven, the vodka hit fast in my system.

"Not a word to your father or Uncle Linkin about last night. We would all be in so much trouble. He would have us going to the prayer meetings at the church for months," Sophia says with a grimace.

I start to laugh. Oh, it hurts! I hold both hands against my temples to try to stop the throbbing.

We are all active in the church. The place of worship downstairs holds two-nights-a-week prayer studies. I love learning about Jesus, but those elders sure like to prolong the time in the room. One night, we were there for three hours, listening to them fuss and mock how today's world is being destroyed by the younger generation.

Aunt Sophia's phone rings from the Bluetooth, sending a lightning bolt of pain through my head.

"How's my girls?" Uncle Linkin's voice booms through the speaker.

Maranda jumps up from her sleep, holding her head. She squints at me. I think vodka is off our menu for a while.

"My head feels like it's in a wood chipper. I can't wait to get home and sleep this pain away."

"Mine too. I just want to go back to sleep and

forget that I have a huge hangover," I whisper so our voices aren't heard over the phone.

Uncle Linkin tells Sophia that Dad and he are heading out to gather some more supplies for the Pilgrims Inn then he will see us at home.

After Sophia hangs up, I scoot down into my seat. I ball up my sweatshirt, laying it against the window then lay my head against it. I slowly drift off to sleep.

I'm startled awake by a knock beside my head. I peek out with the eye closest to the window, and there stands Ruby Lyn holding Bo. He is licking up and down the glass. His nails are raking against it. OMG! The screeching sound is killing me.

I sit up fast, and inside, everything suddenly starts to spin. I get very queasy. When I try to get out of the car, scared I am going to throw up, I stagger back, hitting the side of the car door and sliding down to the ground. I close my eyes and lay my head down on my knees where I now sit.

I can hear Aunt Sophia and Nova talking to me, but I don't want to lift my head, scared everything will start to spin again. I hear a crunching noise. Peeking between my legs, I see men's *Nike* shoes. Since Dad and Linkin are gone, it could only be the one person who has been avoiding me since I chose Iker over him.

"Is she okay?" Az asks.

"Just a little hungover. We did Beer Pong last

night, but vodka was the substitute. She's probably dehydrated," Maranda says. She squats down beside me, sticking her head in between my legs and looking up at me.

"You okay in there?" She laughs.

I nod. Still dizzy, I lift my head slowly. Looking up, I see Az standing there, eyes full of concern. "Can I help you up?" he asks.

Without answering, I just nod. I'm so overwhelmed with what happened at the club. The betrayal from Iker and drinking my sorrows away. I hate myself for hurting Az. My heart feels like it dropped to the bottom of my stomach and broke into a million pieces. I want to just wrap my arms around him and ask him to forgive me, but he deserves better than an apology.

He scoops me up, cradling me to his chest. I cannot help but sniff his shirt. The cologne he wears smells amazing. His strong hands tighten around my body as he carries me to the house.

"I'm sorry," we both say in unison.

I look up at him, and he gives me a smile. "Jinx." He stops at the front door. "Are you okay to stand?"

I nod.

He loosens his hold on me, letting my legs dangle down. He lowers me till my feet are flat on the ground. I gaze up at him. His soft dark brown eyes stare down at me. His fingers curl into my hair, then he traces his hand down my chin. A small shiver runs down my body. I'm completely confused by my body's reaction to his. Iker's touch never made me react this way. I step back. I don't want to rush into anything right now. I just got my heart stomped on.

"Let's go in. I'll tell you all about my birthday bash." I reach out, grabbing his hand and leading him inside.

My phone dings. I reach in my back pocket and pull it out.

Maranda: *I'll see you later. I need ibuprofen and sleep. Oh! Just kiss the boy.*

Me: *Go take a hike.*

Maranda: *Love you, Chica. Don't think, just feel.*

Once inside, I head straight down the foyer then turn right, taking a step up the stairs. I tighten my hand on Az's. I want him to follow me so we can talk. I want this awkwardness gone. I miss him.

As I touch my doorknob, I turn. "I need you." That's all I can say.

12

Az

EMMA LEADS ME to her room where I swore I would never go again. The memory of her telling me she chose Iker over me screws with my head. She broke my heart that day.

My mom always said I had an old-soul heart. I never really had a girlfriend in school. I always looked for a girl who piqued my interest, but no one ever came close to give my heart the flutter. Until now.

Beckham gave me the "don't get involved with my sister because if something happens then things would be difficult when we hang out" speech. He also said that Emma liked bad boys and I was not one of them.

I tried to keep my distance. I stopped coming by the house and started hanging out at the arcade. I hate playing those corny games. But all the talk her brother gave me is thrown out the window when she launches at me, causing us both to fall on the bed.

I'm torn between pushing her off or just listening to my body and kiss her. Emma licks her lips and looks at mine like she's trying to decide if she wants to kiss me too. Her eyes meet mine, and her cheeks turn red from being caught. I decide to give it one more try.

"Can I?" I ask in a low, nervous voice.

"Yes." Her mouth crashes down on mine urgently.

I growl from deep inside, and it kind of scares me. I mean, I'm an adult now, but all these feelings bubbling inside me are not good. I want this girl so bad. I shake the crazy thoughts out and concentrate on my actions.

I run my hand down her side and stop right on her ass. I squeeze. She moans into my mouth. My heart is pounding.

"Az," she whispers.

I sigh and close my eyes to calm down. We are in her house with the door wide open, making out. I'm not this guy. I have respect.

"We can't do this, Emma."

She rolls off me, and I tense. I'm afraid she's going to tell me it was a mistake.

Emma leans up on her elbow, looking at me. She is frowning. "I'm so sorry, Az. I was a total bitch to you. I do have feelings for you, and it scares me. I don't know what I ever saw in Iker, but he is a total jerk-face. I just wanted to be the cool girl for once."

Just seeing the hurt on her face makes me want to go find him and kick his ass. I never understood why girls were attracted to douchebags, but Iker is ranked number one on my radar.

I lean in, kissing her forehead and whisper, "I want to see where we go. We are young and have our whole life ahead of us. Only time can tell. Plus we're going to the same college. If we get tired of each other, then just know I will be here for you no matter what. Deal?"

"I want nothing more than to try, Az. We are young, and I want to just have fun and experience new things. I think everything is going to be okay now." She lies back down on the bed, shifting so her head is on my shoulder.

My phone rings, startling me. I must have dozed off on Emma's bed. She's curled up to my side with her leg thrown over mine. I lift a little, hoping not to wake her, and grab my phone from my front pocket. My mom's name appears on the screen. Crap, my sister.

I pick up immediately. "Hi, mom."

"Look, I got held up at work. Can you and Ruby Lyn hang out at Emma's for a little while? I promise to make it up to you both with Caramel Frappuccinos." She sounds tired.

"Sure, Mom, that sounds great."

After we hang up, Emma sits up, whipping the drool off the side of her mouth. I look down and notice my shirt is wet.

She frowns. "Sorry, I slobbered all over you. I was in a deep sleep."

"I always wanted a girl to drool over my hot body." I chuckle.

She dives on top of me and starts tickling me on my side. I buck her off, rolling on top of her. I start tickling her back. She is laughing and screaming.

"Boy, you better get off my daughter before I kick your ass," Mr. Sparks growls.

I pull away, both of us breathing hard. "Sorry, sir, we were just playing around."

"Not on the bed, you two won't. Now, get up and go help your brother and Ruby Lyn put the volleyball net up. Family time." He turns to walk out.

"That man is scary," I say.

Emma giggles. "He would have been really scary if he saw us asleep earlier." She rolls to her side of the bed and jumps up. "Come on, before he comes back in here with Uncle Linkin."

Well, she doesn't have to tell me twice.

13

Emma

MONDAY MORNING, I lie in bed, looking up at the ceiling. I am dreading going to school. Iker has texted me several times, asking if I would meet up with him to let him explain himself. There is nothing to talk about. He made his bed, and now it's his time to lie in it.

I wonder if everyone at school knows what happened this weekend. Jessica hasn't posted anything on Instagram, which is surprising since her whole life revolves around social media. But I wouldn't put it past her to start spreading damn rumors.

Well, time to get up and put on my big-girl panties and face my troubles. Az and Ruby Lyn are riding with me this morning since their mom didn't get home from work till late. Beckham decided to hitch a ride with this girl he met over the weekend. I feel sorry for whoever falls for him. He doesn't do relationships.

Throwing on a pair of sweats and one of Nova's racecar t-shirts, I head to the bathroom to freshen up. Once I've brushed the grime off my teeth, I pull my hair up into a sloppy bun on top of my head. I look myself over in the mirror. I look decent. I walk out, grabbing my bookbag from beside my bedroom door and tossing it over my shoulder.

I make it down the stairs and stop. Dad's holding a plate of chocolate pop tarts. He hands it to me. "Here, pumpkin. Nova said this will give you energy."

"Thanks, Dad." Nova came in last night and lay in the bed with me until I fell asleep. She told me that tomorrow at school might be bad but to hold my head high and not listen to anyone.

So, I guess the junk food is supposed to make me feel better.

"Do I have something to worry about with you and Az? I mean, you were just sneaking out, trying to meet that troubled boy from school, and now Az? I just want to know where you two stand with each other."

"No, Dad. We are just friends. That's all." I head out the door before anything else is said.

"Emma, look at me," Ruby Lyn hollers while she does a cartwheel in our front yard.

She slips and slides, rolling down the hill. Max

pushes by me, running over to place his body over hers. He starts to lick her all over her face. She starts to squeal and tries to push him off.

I rush over, followed by everyone else. Ruby Lyn has her hands around Max and is giggling while she tries to get up. "Did you see me, Emma?"

"Girl, you trying to give us a heart attack?" Uncle Linkin says, grabbing Max by the collar and pulling him off her.

"Nope. I was just showing Emma what I have learned to do."

I brush off the leaves on her clothes and fix her hair. "Okay, silly girl, it's time to go to school. You hurt anywhere?" I ask.

"I'm fine." She laughs, running toward the car. "Shotgun!" she hollers over her shoulder.

Lord, she is wired this morning. I need some of that energy. I wonder what is taking Az so long to get ready. I look down at my watch. Crap, I need to be going now.

As I walk toward the car, I catch a glimpse of Az walking through the grass, heading towards me. I can't help but notice he looks different. He is wearing a pair of dark-washed jeans that hang low off his hips and a tight navy long-sleeve shirt showing off his muscular chest. There's no denying that I'm gawking at him. I may have even drooled a bit.

I shake my head to get the sexual thoughts I have out. We are friends for now. I know for sure all the girls at school will be chasing after him now. He is hot with a capital H.

He finally makes it over to the car and gives me a one-arm hug. "Hey, sorry, I was running late. I just got out of the shower." He lets go of me to open the car door.

Ruby Lyn rolls the window down. "I get to sit in the front seat." She is smiling big.

"Squirt, you're pushing my patience, but since you got yourself ready and ate breakfast, I'm going to let this one slide." Az shuts her door and gets in the back.

He folds his arms, and his lips push out. I grin. He is pouting. "All right, everyone, seat belts on. If you would please tip your driver when the ride is over."

Az flips me off, and Ruby Lyn's eyes get wide with shock. I turn the key in the ignition. Okay, time to get this day over with.

After dropping her off, Az jumps up front. "Can you believe in three more months we will be done with school? I can't wait to get out of here and be on my own. I love my family, but I'm so ready to have a teenage life."

"Oh, you have no idea how much I'm done with this town." I groan, turning my blinker on and heading into the school parking lot.

"I'm sure you are. Well, not too much longer." He winks at me.

This boy is so cute. He sits, halfway turned toward me, with a big, broad smile. He looks down at my lips and back at me. I have fantasized about his soft, thick lips since our first encounter.

I take the opportunity to unfasten my seat belt and lean into the center console; he scoots closer too. Our lips are just a few inches apart. His fresh, clean scent fills my nostrils, sending chill bumps down my arms. The attraction I have to his smell is odd, but I really like it.

I open my lips and lick them. I move closer and let my moist lips touch his. Az opens slightly, and I let my tongue enter slowly. The passion of our tongues gliding together clouds my brain. I want more of him. I continue to possess his mouth. I wrap my arms around his neck, bringing him closer to me. Minutes later, our kiss is ended by a loud beating sound from the window on his side.

"Gross! Get out of the car, and no making out again." Beckham's voice comes in muffled from outside.

I open my eyes, and my brother has his face smashed against the glass. Why me? Why did God give me an irritating brother? A slight breeze blows on my face. I know Mom is here.

Sorry, Mom! I do love him. He is just a little odd.

A piece of my hair moves, and I know she is playing with it. I remember sitting on her lap while she twirled her fingers through my hair while we watched *Mickey Mouse Clubhouse*. Dad said I would be out like a light and never made it to the end of the show.

I sigh, thinking about those memories.

"Come on, sis. It's time to show them you're not scared of no one." He taps the window with one of the crutches.

Good Lord, let me get out before he breaks my window.

★ ★ ★

I ARRIVE HOME with a throbbing headache. Iker texted me repeatedly during class. I finally had to block his number. Pulling in the driveway, I'm met with Dad standing on the porch. Once I get the door open, Max comes pounding down the driveway, wagging his tail.

"Hey, boy." I kneel, scratching him behind his ears.

I stand and make my way down the walkway with Max in tow. When I get to the porch, Dad steps down and wraps me in a big hug.

"Hey, kitten. How was your day?" He rubs my back.

Okay, am I on hidden camera? Dad hasn't been

this affectionate since I was a child. As I got older, it's been more bossing me around and telling me how irresponsible I am and how I don't help with the chores around the house. Crap, someone died.

"Oh my God, who went to heaven? Are Grandma and Grandpa okay?" I quickly pull away, wrapping my arms around myself with worry.

They're the only thing I have left of my mom, except for my aggravating brother. Who, by the way, is going to get a knuckle sandwich when he gets home.

"No one died. I wanted to spend some time with you. I really didn't get to see much of you on your birthday. Plus, I have a birthday gift I have been waiting to give you." He links our arms together as he leads me into the house.

We make it into the den where a large box sits, wrapped in Minnie Mouse birthday paper. I have to laugh.

"Dad, I'm not three anymore."

"Baby girl, in my eyes, you will always be little. Now go take a seat and unwrap it."

I run over, so excited to open it. I love presents, but who doesn't? I slide my finger across the taped part of the paper. The crinkling of the wrapping echoes in my ear. I rip some more until a brown cardboard box is showing. There is no picture or writing on it to tell me what it is.

FLAWLESS REBELLION

I shake the big box, but no sound comes from it. Dad laughs. "Let me cut the plastic." He pulls out his army knife he always carries around and slices the tape. "I've waited a long time to give this to you. Grief is a powerful thing, and I wanted to make sure you could handle what's inside."

He pops the top two large pieces of the cardboard open, and I lean down to peek inside. I reach in with both hands, pulling out a large quilt. I unravel the ribbon it's tied with, holding it out so I can see it all.

The cover is made of t-shirts lined with a camouflage border. "These are your mom's t-shirts. I saved them for you and Beckham for a sentimental gift. This shirt here?" Dad says, pointing to the one in the center. He pulls it closer so I can see it. The shirt is gray and, on the upper left side, has an eagle with its wings spread wide, holding an American flag. "This was one of your mother's favorite shirts in the navy. She wore this to take her morning runs. If you put your nose up to it and close your eyes, you will be able to smell her scent."

I pull it up close and take a deep sniff. I quickly notice a faint scent of vanilla and brown sugar. Tears escape down my face and course under my chin. I can smell my mom. At that very moment, I feel Dad's arms wrap around me, rocking me from where I dropped to my knees on the floor.

"It's like she is still here. I remember sitting on her lap and her playing with my hair." The moisture from my tears seeps through the top of my shirt. I didn't know you could cry that much. My whole body is shaking.

"Shush, honey, I didn't mean to upset you. I just wanted to give you something special." Dad's voice trembles. "I really loved your mom. I followed her around on base, but she never once noticed me, but when she was thrown from a bomb, I made a promise I was going to fight to get her. The day I came to her home to take care of her, our love grew."

I have been so curious about why Uncle Linkin and Dad were living with Mom before Aunt Sophia came. I wonder if Mom loved Linkin first. I've got to ask.

"Hey, Dad. Can I ask you something? Please don't get mad."

He pulls away, wiping his eyes. Sitting cross-legged on the floor, he just looks at me, waiting for my question.

"Was Momma in love with Uncle Linkin? Is that why she didn't notice you?" I ask.

His eyes widen. Dad clears his throat. "As a matter of fact, she was. When your uncle arrived on base. She couldn't keep her eyes off him. One night, your mom was dealing with a lot of demons in her life, and she went for a run in the woods. Linkin went for a hike also. He noticed your mom was upset. I don't know all that was said, but he made it clear his heart was somewhere else. After that, they became great friends."

Dad didn't say any more. He stood up and offered his hand to help me up. I know when he is overthinking stuff, and the look he is giving me tells me he wants to say more. Once standing, I pick my blanket back up and place it in the box. I'll lay it on my bed later.

"Okay, kitten. Time for homemade pizza and garlic knots." He gives a slight smile, collects the scattered paper on the ground, and heads to the kitchen.

I really need to do some snooping in Dads' closet. I know he keeps some of Mom's personal stuff hidden in a box covered with a quilt.

14

Emma

I FINALLY BUILT up the courage to sneak into Dads' room. The deadline for sending all my college information to Clemson is in a week. On the application, it asks for my social security number, Mom's and Dad's information, and a shot record.

A month has passed, and things have been going great. Az and I have grown closer, sharing things about each other. He came over today so we can both finish our paperwork then head out to meet Maranda and her new guy.

"Is this the box you were talking about?" Az asks, holding the hidden treasure from the top shelf of the closet.

I smile. "That's it."

Az walks over and hands it to me. I flip off the top, rummaging through a lot of papers. I flip fast until I stop at a newspaper clipping that says, "Three-year-old girl survived being kidnapped by rapist father and sold for money."

That's weird. Why would that be in there? I sit it down beside me on the floor and go back to sorting through the papers.

"You know, you could just ask your dad where your stuff is. He had this stuff put up for a reason, and we shouldn't be snooping," Az says from the doorway while making sure no one comes in.

"I have this gut feeling they are hiding something from me. I feel like I don't belong sometimes."

Az looks at me, eyebrows raised with curiosity. "Do you really want to know? I have learned some things just need to be kept hidden."

I turn back to the box, my mind focusing on the thick papers stuffed inside. I need to know what is in here. I know Az is right, but I am overwhelmed with all these feelings coursing through me. I feel that something inside will reveal a hidden secret about me.

I notice a small pink photo album sitting at the bottom. Reaching in, I pick it up and open it to the first page. Intensely, I stare down at the picture of my mom in a hospital room, looking down at a baby lying on her chest. Mom is smiling, but mascara smears down her face from crying.

I look up quickly. "Az, my dad is not in the picture. Is that not a little strange? He was there when Beckham was born."

"Like I said, snooping is not going to get you anywhere, just a lot of questions. Why don't you just ask him or Linkin?"

I sigh. "They both just beat around the bush. I never get the whole story. I can promise you there is something in here that will tell me what they are hiding."

Az rubs my back. "Okay, well, let me help." He reaches over and grabs a stack of papers from the back side.

★ ★ ★

AFTER THIRTY MINUTES of flipping through tons of paperwork about Mom's discharge after the bomb in Alaska, I come across a blue-and-gray paper: a certificate of birth.

"I found it!" I hold it to my chest.

My heart is beating so fast, and I start to shake.

"Emma, you are trembling." Az wraps his arms around me, holding tightly.

I just close my eyes and surrender into his arms. I have waited for this moment. I want to reassure myself that my worrying is nothing. And now, I have it right here, against me.

"Come on, let's get off the floor." He gets up and

reaches out his hand to help me up.

My hands start to sweat and tremble while I start skimming down my certificate. I see my name, but my last name is not the same as Dad's.

"That's weird," I say.

Az leans in, looking at the paper. "What is?"

I don't get it. Why would Dad not be on my birth certificate? I read on down, and where the father is supposed to sign, there is no signature. I start to tear up, and my stomach feels queasy.

"Look, Az. My father didn't sign my birth certificate, and my last name is the same as Mom's."

My heart is racing, and my legs start to go numb. I know it's my anxiety hitting. I'm not my father's daughter.

I can't breathe. I try to stand up, but my legs give out, and I collapse on the floor. I wince. I take deep breaths to push away this pain in my chest. Az kneels in front of me, his face full of worry. His hands rake over my body, checking me out.

"What happened? Where do you hurt?" he asks with concern.

"I'm fine. I got worked up with what I just found. I had a panic attack." I take in a few deep breaths.

I can't wrap my mind around my birth certificate. I saw Dad's signature on Beckham's, so why didn't he sign mine? I reach for the scattered papers I dropped when I fell.

"Come on, let's go to your room. You can go through them there. With our luck, your dad or uncle will pop in here, and we'll both get in trouble," Az says, wrapping his arm around my body and leading me out.

I feel like my legs have weights on them. I'm confused more than before, and I hate this feeling. I slowly drag myself to the bed. Az waits for me to sit on the edge then rests beside me.

"All right, let's go through these and get them back before anyone knows they are missing. There's got to be something in here that will explain the birth certificate." He sighs.

We read through the article about the kidnapping. A large photo shows an old beat-up house with missing shutters. Cops are surrounding it, and yellow tape is wrapped around the whole place. I continue to read the article. My name pops up as the daughter of Kyle Bumgardner, who took the child and was planning to sell her for money.

Wait a minute. I must have read that wrong. I read it again, thinking it was just my imagination, but there, in clear black ink, is written Emma Armstrong. Next to a picture of me in my Minnie Mouse outfit.

I skim the paragraphs, reading about the kidnapping. Mom's name appears on down. It talks about how she was raped a long time ago by two men and got pregnant. I start to laugh hysterically. "Of course, I was conceived by rape," I say through tears and laughter.

I think I'm going insane.

I feel a brush of air hit my face. I shake my head. I can feel my mom's presence.

"How could you lie to me? I bet Dad, Uncle Linkin, Aunt Sophia, Nova, and Mamaw and Papaw knew too. Are you shitting me right now?"

I turn around, my face burning hot. I'm so mad right now my hands are shaking badly. A piece of paper falls from in between the newspaper clippings.

Joint Custody Agreement

Agreement between Linkin Garland and Malcom Sparks. The family members of the minor child listed below agree they will serve as joint custodians and will jointly discuss and determine all major decisions concerning the child.

"Look, Emma, I think you need to go talk with your dad and uncle. Let them explain—" Az says, but I throw my hand in front of his face. I don't want to hear a word he's saying.

My eyes are glassy from tears. I want to just run away.

"You know what, Az? Just go home. I need to be

alone." I point to the door.

"I don't think that's a good idea." He steps towards me.

I step back. I don't want his touch now. I want to get away from this life that was a lie. "Out!" I shout loudly.

Az jerks back and gapes at me. But he doesn't move closer to me. He turns and walks out.

A few minutes pass before I hear the door slam. I rush over to my closet and grab a bookbag. I begin to throw some clothes, panties, bras, toiletry items, my e-cigs, and the hidden cash from chores I did around the house.

Life is such a bitch.

I barely make it outside the front door before Aunt Sophia calls my name. I storm out, snatching my keys from the side table. The cool air hits me in the face as I'm running fast to the car. My whole body is trembling. I'm not sure if it's from the cold or the fact I found out that both my parents are dead.

15

Az

"So, explain to me again why Emma needed her personal stuff to fill out her form for college. We told her we would do that tonight and fill it out together," Mr. Sparks asks, taking a seat in front of me in their kitchen.

Linkin and Sophia sit down as well. She slides a blueberry muffin and a soda in front of me.

I smile. "Thank you."

They all are just sitting here, looking right at me, waiting for me to talk. I hate being in the middle of this family issue.

I clear my throat and sit up straight. "Emma said she has been feeling out of place here for a while now. She said she felt like you were hiding something."

"I don't understand how she could feel that way. We have always treated Emma like a little princess.

She was always placed on a pedestal since I met her," Linkin says.

"I'm speechless. She is my daughter and will always be. I have never acted any differently." Malcom leans his elbows on the table, looking sad.

I don't know what to say here. I'm just a neighbor and a friend. I don't even know how to explain Emma's feelings. This family loves her very much. To me, they were just more overprotective than most parents.

"Look, all I know is Emma kept saying something was off. She noticed you hid a box in your closet, so she went snooping. The stuff she found was disturbing. No offense, but she is eighteen now and should have been told," I admit, shaking my head.

I can't believe I blurted that out. As a teenager myself, if I found out that my parents lied to me about my life, I would be pissed too. There comes a time when the truth should be told. Lies just end up hurting everyone involved.

"Az, we didn't hold this information to hurt her. Darcy never wanted Emma to know who her real father was. When she was kidnapped by her father, it was the scariest thing for me. I would die for my daughter. She is my child even if our DNA is not the same. I'm her father." He pushes back from the table, and the chair squeals loudly.

He walks over to the window and braces his hands tightly against the counter, his breathing ragged. "I promised Darcy I would protect her, and that's what I've been doing. I never wanted her to feel pain. But now, her finding out this God-awful news is crushing my heart."

As I watch how upset everyone is, I know this must have been hard on them. Linkin is a preacher, and for him to hold this truth from Emma, it must have been bad.

"You all did what you thought was right. She needs to hear the truth from all of you. Let her cool down. I'll go look for her and bring her back here."

"Thank you," Sophia comes around the table to hug me tightly around the neck. "Please tell her we do love her. We never wanted to hide this from her. We only honored her mother's wishes."

I squeeze her arms in comfort. "Sophia, she knows you love her, and she loves you. Nothing is going to change that. Emma is just in shock and hurt right now. I'll be back shortly." I stand and turn to leave.

"Az."

As soon as Mr. Sparks utters my name, I turn around. He stands there, still where he was. "You tell Emma that no matter what, she is my daughter. God placed her in my life to be her dad," he says, choking up as he speaks.

"I sure will, sir." I turn and make my way out.

My phone chimes, and I grab it out of my pocket. It's a text from Maranda.

Maranda: Emma is wasted and left with Iker to a party. I couldn't stop her. Come get me.

Dammit. I'm pissed now. How can she keep running back to this douche? I should just go home and let her deal with her sadness on her own. I get to the house, and I'm glad Mom is home. I'll just tell her I have to pick up Emma from Maranda's and be right back.

Again, here I am, being the rug she uses to brush her feet off. Once she is safely home, I'm throwing in the towel. I need someone who puts me first for once.

About ten minutes later, Maranda and I walk down the crowded sidewalk bordered with cars and leading to a fraternity party. Music throbs around us as we walk in the open door of this huge house.

"This place is crowded. I don't know how we are going to find her in here," Maranda hollers against the noise.

"We are going to scope out this whole place until we find her. Iker better hope when I do, his hands are nowhere near her."

I tell myself repeatedly to stay calm, but after thirty minutes of not finding Emma, I start to panic. The last place I haven't checked is upstairs. I push my way through the crowd, heading for the stairs. Maranda comes around the corner to meet me. She is breathing heavily like she's been for a run.

"I just ran into Jessica in the kitchen. She said Emma is wasted. Emma and Iker have been doing shots for about an hour. Jessica said the last time she saw them, they were in the living room, dancing seductively together."

I rush up the stairs, opening the first door I see. When I look in, I sigh with relief. It's just the bathroom. I walk down the hallway, opening each door, but find them all empty.

There's one more room left. I hear a squeaking noise coming through the door. I jiggle the doorknob, and it's locked, like I expected. I step back to give myself enough room so I can kick the door in.

"Did he fuck you, Emma?" Iker's voice comes from behind the door.

I bend my knee and kick hard above the doorknob. There's a cracking noise, but the door is still locked. I kick one more time, and the door slams open.

Emma lies naked on the bed, not moving. I look around the room for Iker. The window across from me is still closed, so I know he is in here.

"Are you looking for me?" Iker steps out from behind the door, holding a beer bottle.

I watch his hand. He thinks he's quick, but I'm quicker. My uncle was a boxing coach over in the Philippines. Over at home, the guys see boxing as a golden ticket out of poverty. I practiced with some mean-ass men over there. Iker is just a baby doll compared to them.

I keep my eye on him, ready for him to make his move. He steps forward with this wicked grin. Bastard. He swings.

I snap. I draw my arm back, balling my fist up. All the anger I have been holding in goes behind the punch I throw at him. When my fist connects under his jaw hard, he stumbles back, looking at me confused, but then he falls, hitting the floor on his back.

"Damn it, son," Malcom says from behind me before walking around me and looking at Iker.

I look over at Emma, making sure she is okay. Maranda is putting her clothes on. She is still out.

"How did you know where we were, sir?"

He glances over at Emma. "I protect my children. Let's just say, if I ever need to find either one of them, I will. I have my secrets from my days in the army. Ones I'll take with me to my death," he says as he gazes at me with a stern look.

"What did he do to her?" Nova rushes through the door, dropping on the bed and looking over Emma.

"I called the cops. They are on the way," Maranda

tells Nova.

Just then, we hear a loud noise from downstairs and the music stops.

"This is the police. Open up."

"Upstairs, sir," someone says.

The room fills with police officers. Some head towards Emma, and the others stop to talk to Malcom. He pulls them over to the side, out of my earshot. As they talk, they look over my way.

My palms start to sweat. I rub them down the front of my jeans. I stiffen when two policemen head my way.

"So, Malcom says that you broke the door in when you heard a noise? When you saw Iker on top of this lady, trying to rape her, you pushed him off her. That's when he swung to hit you. Is this how it happened?" he asks, writing it down in his little notebook. "Then you hit him in self-defense?" he continues, never once looking up at me.

"Yes, sir."

That's all I can say.

After more questioning and the ambulance arriving to look over Emma, they take her to the hospital to be checked out.

16

Emma

I FEEL A hand softly brush the hair from my face, and soft lips kiss my forehead. "My sweet girl! You scared the shit out of me. Yes, your Aunt Sophia can say bad words too."

I feel the bed dip down beside me. I try to open my eyes, but they are so heavy. My whole body feels so heavy, like someone is holding me down. I hear this God-awful beeping sound coming from above my head. It's sending severe pain to the top of my forehead. God, someone please shut the noise off.

"Knock, knock!" a female voice calls out. "Can I come in?"

"Yes," someone answers. It might be Nova, but I'm not sure since the woman's voice is so faint.

I try to open my eyes again. I squeeze tightly then push my eyebrows up, hoping this will help. I see a bright light, shining above and making my head pound. I lift my hand to block it and wait a few minutes before I glance around.

"Hey, sweetie," Aunt Sophia says quietly.

"Good, you're awake. You scared the shit out of me, Emma. Don't do it again." Nova comes around to the other side of the bed and takes my hand. Hers feel like ice.

"Sorry. I was so mad," I say in a raspy voice.

"I know you were. Your family has a lot to talk to you about." Her tone is soothing now.

The doctor clears her voice. "I need to take a listen, and then she will be discharged. The medicine has worn off now."

What is she talking about? Why did I need drugs?

Sophia and Nova both squeeze my hands and walk out of the room. I'm starting to panic. I don't know why I am here. I think hard about what I was doing before being here.

"I'm Dr. Swanton. You've been asleep for ten hours straight. Do you remember anything about what happened to you?"

I scramble around in my mushy brain, trying to remember what I did. Shit! The party.

"I went to a frat party. I was upset with my family and went to have some fun. I remember playing a drinking card game, but after that, nothing."

I neglect to tell her I smoked some pot. She might frown upon me.

"After some blood work and a urine test from your catheter, it shows a lot of drugs were put in your system all at once. That is why you can't remember anything."

I stare at her in shock. I didn't do any other drugs. What is she talking about?

I shake my head. "I didn't want to tell you, so please don't tell my parents, but I smoked marijuana."

I start to get nauseated. My dad is going to skin me alive when he finds out. Oh, he is not my father. I have a fake family. Beckham is my half-brother, but other than Mom's parents, I'm alone.

"Well, that did show up, but you also had high traces of benzodiazepine and cocaine. After speaking with the authorities, the boy you were with admitted lacing your drinks with it. He also used a sleep aid called Ambien, which is why you were passed out."

"What!" I cry out.

I'm shaking all over.

"Good news is he didn't rape you. I examined you, and everything is still intact. I drew a few more labs just as a precaution, and once they are back and everything looks good, I will release you." Dr. Swanton pats my hand and turns to leave.

"Will you not tell my family about me smoking?" I

ask nervously.

I want to make a clean slate. I promise to never do anything like this again. I just want my life back. My real one.

"Emma, you are considered an adult. Under HIPPA, we cannot disclose any information about you unless you authorize it. But as a mother of children, I would want to know if my kids were using." She gives me a sad smile and walks out the door.

My stomach drops at her words. She is right, my mother would be crushed if she saw me right now. I truly believe the reason she hasn't left me is because she knew, one day, I would find out I was born out of rape. How could she allow me to be born from such a disgusting man?

"I hate you!" I cry out loud.

I sit up and throw my legs over the hospital bed. I just want to hit someone. I jump down and stumble on the cold porcelain floor. The room is spinning, but I don't care. I reach over to grab the telephone that sits beside the bed. Without caring, I snatch the cord out of the wall and throw the phone, hitting the mirror in front of me.

Glass shatters and flies around me. I just stand there and look at the little pieces of mirror left standing. That's me: broken in half. I can only see my nose and mouth. Nothing else exists. I'm just a hollowed, broken girl, who is left on earth alone.

I feel movement and then hands cover my face. "What happened? Are you okay?" Nova whispers.

I open my eyes, looking straight at her. Her face is red and blotchy with tears falling down her cheeks. I haven't seen her cry like this before. At that moment, I let out all of my tears I have been fighting to hold in.

"I can't take this anymore. I feel like I'm suffocating."

"Ma'am, we need to check your abrasions." Two nurses start examining me.

★ ★ ★

AN HOUR LATER, I'm released from the hospital. I had to promise Dr. Swanton I would see a therapist before she would allow me to leave. Now I sit in the back of Nova's Hot Rod car with Uncle Linkin on one side and Dad on the other. Neither of them has spoken a word to me. I crouch down, pulling my feet up on the seat and let sleep take over.

I wake to a loud thumping sound, and I open my eyes. We are sitting in the driveway at home. Dad opens the car door and gets out.

"Let's get into the house before the bottom drops out from the sky."

Dark clouds hover above me when I step out. I walk toward the house, taking quick look over at Az's house, but there's no movement that I can see from here.

I climb the steps with my head down, and suddenly, I plow into a body.

"Hey, sis. Sorry I wasn't there at the hospital, but Dad said I wasn't allowed."

"Seriously, Beckham. Watch where you are standing." I charge forward, throwing the door open on my way in.

I have nothing to say to him right now. I know he was the one who snitched on me and told Dad where I was. I was lucky Az found me, or things would have been worse, but to have my dad see me lying on the bed naked and drugged embarrasses me.

"Take a seat, Emma, we have lots of talking to do," Dad says, pointing to the couch.

I take a seat. I fold my hands in my lap, waiting to listen to what each one of them has to say.

"I'm going to go first because it started with me," Aunt Sophia blurts out.

She looks over at Uncle Linkin with sadness. He reaches for her hand.

"I was living with my boyfriend years ago. He was in the army. I was so excited that we had our own place. One night, we were watching TV, snuggled on the couch. Brad told me he needed to go to the restroom." She took a deep breath and let it out. "I fell asleep waiting on him to come back.

"I awoke to a noise. I went looking for Brad, thinking he had fallen and got hurt. When I got to the room, he had a gun in his hand." Her hands are trembling. Uncle Linkin reaches over and tightens his large hand around hers.

I can tell something bad happened. I wonder if I should tell her it's okay. I can wait until later to get more information about what I found.

"Anyway, Brad threatened to kill me. I tried to run, but he hit me with the weapon and knocked me out. When I awoke, I had been cut bad, and he had raped me. After being beaten again when I tried to escape, I decided, even if it took my life, I was going to get away. I pretended to be knocked out from when he beat me with his fist. When he moved away from me, I jumped up and ran as fast as I could. I threw my body over the fence and hit the grass. I got up quickly and made it down the street to the neighbor's house."

Listening to my aunt tell this horror story that happened to her is breaking my heart.

"I'm so sorry…" I say in a whisper.

Uncle Linkin clears his throat. "I was the chaplain who was called to pray over her. When I arrived at the hospital, I felt a pull to Sophia. Since I counsel soldiers with PTSD and their spouses, a friend of mine asked me to help her.

"I got called on a mission in Alaska, so I had to do our session on Skype. So, when I arrived on base. I met Malcom and your mother. Your mother was a sharp woman and taught us how to get in shape."

He lets out a breath. "I had a lot on my mind that day, so I took a run up a mountain. I ran into your mother. She was upset."

For a few minutes, he doesn't say a word. I watch his Adam's apple bob in his throat. I know that what he is about to say is going to be bad.

"Darcy seemed upset, so I told her to come see me so we could talk. See, your mother made a move on me, but I bluntly told her I was in love with someone else. Your mom let out a lot that night that she'd been holding in for a long time. What I am about to tell you is going to be very disturbing."

I stiffen. "Okay."

I sit there and wait... and wait, but he just looks at me so sadly. It must be bad if he can't talk about it. Uncle Linkin has heard and seen some horrific things in his line of work, and for him to linger, it must be very upsetting.

"What I am about to tell you, your mother never wanted you to know. She never once wanted you to think you were never loved. Understand?"

I frown. Now I'm curious about what happened to my mom.

He clears his throat. "When I saw your mother so upset, I knew something was wrong, because she was always smiling. We sat down, and she told me about a time when she went dancing."

He looks over to Dad, and Dad nods his head.

"Your mom decided to dance between two guys on the dance floor. It was a fast song. Somehow, she didn't pay attention, and they had gotten to the edge near an exit door. They dragged her out the door where they both raped her."

"What!?" I scream. "My mom was raped by two men?"

I just can't believe this. My heart hurts, and it feels like it's breaking into millions of pieces. I start swiping away at the tears that stream down my face.

"Did Mom regret me? She didn't even want me, did she?" I yell out, throwing my arms up in the air.

I want to run away. I don't know how much more I can take.

Dad wraps his arms around me, and I try to wiggle out, but he is too strong for me.

"Your mother loved you. She told us both that two wrongs don't make a right. At first, she was furious, but then she realized all the anger was for the two guys, and they needed to be punished for what they did. Once your mother got everything off her chest, she was at peace. Never doubt the love your mother had for you. You understand? She never regretted you."

My face is so hot and sticky from all the crying. Aunt Sophia hands me a tissue. I blow my nose, making this God-awful hooting noise. Everyone laughs, including me.

"The article I found. My dad kidnapped me and was going to sell me for money?" I ask.

"Yes," Dad says abruptly. "We were at the park when I heard a loud pop from a balloon. When I turned back around, a man had you in his arms. He ran to a car that was waiting for him. Your father had been watching us." His voice is trembling.

Listening to him tell the rest of the story, I understand. Nova, Dad, and Uncle Linkin put their life on the line for me. I know now why they kept this from me.

"That's why you both have joint custody of me. Mom wanted to make sure we all stayed together as a family."

"You're completely right, honey. Some of us are not blood kin, but that is not what makes a family. It's the love we all share for one another, and those who accept you for who you are that matters most." Nova walks over to me, squatting down so she is looking me in the eyes. "You might not be mine, but I raised you as my own. I will always love you, no matter what."

She wraps me into a hug.

Everyone gets up, and we are all crammed into a big embrace.

"All right, enough making my sister cry. I'm the only one that can do that. Oh, I ordered pizza, breadsticks, brownies, and wings."

"Wow, I'm impressed. Where did you get the money?" Dad asks.

"Oh, I have your credit card on file on my Papa John's app."

Dad glares at him, and we all just burst out in laughter. Leave it to my brother to turn a depressing matter into a hilarious one.

17

Emma

THE FOLLOWING WEEKS got better. School agreed to let me do my assignments from home. I have one more week until graduation. Nova has slept in my room every night since the horrific incident. Iker is still in custody but will appear in front of the judge in a couple of days. Our lawyer told us he will be charged as an adult since he is eighteen. He might not be sentenced for long, but he will have to do at least two years of community service and see a therapist. I was scared he would come after me, but he is not allowed within a hundred feet of me ever.

I try to text Az every day. I miss him so much. I walked over to his house a couple of days after being back from the hospital, but no one was home. I am outside on the porch, reading a book when I see his mom pull up. I throw my book down and run over to the car. She opens her door and frowns.

"Az is not here. Both kids missed their yaya, so they both flew home two weeks ago. They are arriving back next weekend."

"I see. I'll talk to him when he gets home." I turn to walk back home.

I can't believe he just left like that, without a goodbye.

I get halfway across the lawn when Marjorie, his mom, calls my name. When I turn, she walks towards me.

"Az told me what happened. He was really shaken up about that fella trying to rape you. You two are still young and have your whole life ahead of you, but I can tell you that when my boy loves someone, he loves with all his heart. Give him time, Emma." She pulls me into a hug then pulls away with a smile. "Good luck with your finals."

"Thank you."

★ ★ ★

TODAY IS GRADUATION day. I have rolled on my deodorant four times now. I look in the mirror for the first time since the day in the hospital. I no longer feel broken. I love my family and I love myself. I've been a little sad since Az refuses to talk to me, but I have backed off and no longer text him.

"Emma!" Dad hollers from downstairs. "We are going to be late. Get your butt down here."

"Coming."

My phone dings inside my pocketbook. I pull it out and see I have a text from Az.

Az: *I'm sorry. :(We need to talk after graduation.*

After all this time, he texts now. He wouldn't even look at me when he got home. I made a fool of myself running over there like a lovesick girl, screaming his name when the cab dropped them off at the house. Not once did he acknowledge me. He walked straight to the door, dragging Ruby Lyn by her hand.

Me: *Who is this?*

I wait for his reply. I can see the three dots showing he is typing.

Az: *I'm the guy who loves you. I was the one who saved you from that asshole. Meet me in the gym, behind the bleacher that doesn't close.*

Wow. He had to bring that up. I'm glad he saved me from being raped, though.

Later on, I found out it was Maranda who told him where I was. Dad told me the earrings I wear have a tracking device in them, so it led him straight to the frat house.

We pull up at the school. Since we are a small graduation class, they are having it outside, in the football stadium. Maranda waves us down at the entrance.

My stomach is in knots over what Az wants to talk about. I'm confused that he told me he loves me, but he ran off because he was upset with what happened.

When we walk into the stadium, I'm escorted to my group. I slide on my gown then place my hat on top of my head.

"This is the most uncomfortable clothing ever." Maranda yanks down the robe like a dress.

"I know, right? Only one hour, and this scratchy cotton material is being thrown in the trash."

"Girls, come on. It's time to line up," Mrs. Scone says, waving to us.

My feet are killing me. I've been waiting for forty-five minutes for my turn to be called. I stand on my tiptoes, looking over everyone's head, trying to find him. He should be next to go across the stage. The principal calls out his name: Az Gacusan Phillips. I hear whistles and applause. I smile big. He did it. He is now a graduate.

The line continues to move. There's one more person ahead of me, and I will be getting my diploma. I'm so excited to leave and make my own path at Clemson. Things have gotten back to normal around the house. My grandparents were not happy Dad didn't tell them about the frat house, but after they found out I knew about the secret everyone was hiding, they left it alone.

"Emma Sparks," I hear. I skip up the stairs, smiling.

It feels good to hold the square piece of paper. I look out to the crowd when I hear a loud whistle. "That's our girl. Way to go, baby," Uncle Linkin and Dad shout from the back.

I skip to the stairs, reciting, "I did it, I did it." I step down, turning to head to my chair.

I felt a warm breeze touch my face. I smile. I know it's Mom. I whisper, "I thought you left me."

A yellow and black butterfly lands on my hand. The wings are beautiful with vibrant yellow patterns. I take a seat then lift my hand closer to my face. The fragile God's creation doesn't fly away. The little legs start to tickle when it moves a little more.

All the commotion around me disappears. It's so quiet. I continue to watch the beautiful creature, hoping this is Mom. I can feel her presence just like when I was three. That's really the only thing I remember about her: when she kissed my fingers and told me she loved me to the moon. The older I get, the more I forget about it and it seems more like a dream.

A piece of my hair moves, and I feel a soft touch.

"Never doubt my love for you. The day you came into my life, you filled the empty hole in my heart. Don't ever worry about not being loved, because I love you with all my heart. I will be watching you from above. Congratulations, baby girl."

The butterfly wisps up in the air. After a minute, clapping noises echo in my ears. I look around to see if anyone is staring, but my fellow classmates are looking straight ahead.

I let out a deep breath and smile. My heart is no longer hurting. It feels full.

She never regretted me.

The second the last classmate is called, I jump up and run down the aisle towards my family, throwing my arms around Dad. "I'm sorry. Please forgive me." I cry.

"Ssh. What's this about? Did something happen?" Dad says, looking concerned.

"No, I just wanted to let you know I'm sorry for being such a brat."

Everyone surrounds us with worry on their face. I squirm out of Dad's arms. "Today I got my closure from Mom. You are all my family, and I love you all very much. Thank you for loving me even when I was not lovable."

"What do you mean by that about Mom?" Beckham asks with balled fists.

This is the first time I have ever seen my brother act this way. "Mom was here today. A butterfly landed on my hand, and I know it was her. She congratulated me and told me to never doubt her love for me."

"This is bullshit," he says, turning and walking away.

I'll deal with him later. He has had some seriously crazy mood swings lately.

★ ★ ★

THE SMELL OF Parmesan hits my senses. I got to pick the restaurant, so here we are, at Gravy's. Nova invited Az and his family.

"Hey. I missed you." Az walks over, wrapping his arms around me.

I close my eyes because it feels good to be held by him again. I've missed this. I draw closer to him, feeling a strong connection.

"Come on, let's eat. I'm hungry," Az says, turning us and leading us to the table.

Our families are already seated, looking at their menus. Nova looks up with a smile and winks.

Dinner goes well. All the adults talk about having a big cook-out the weekend before we head to look at Clemson campus. We are going to head down that morning and then camp at lake Jocassee. They are going to rent a cabin and a boat so we can go explore the waterfalls. I'm hoping the conversation with Az goes well. I know we are just starting a new chapter in our life. College is a big step for us and we've both agreed to just be friends, but I can't picture my life without him.

Life is like an umbrella. Sometimes we choose to keep our guard up to protect us from getting wet. But the rain never hurt anyone. It's just inconvenient. I am ready to leave my past, my umbrella, behind and learn to dance in the rain.

Hopefully, Az is too.

18

Emma

I DROP DOWN at the end of the bed and scoot so I can sit Indian style. "I can't believe they allowed us to talk in my room," I say.

"Your father and I had a discussion after what happened," Az says, never losing eye contact. "I told him how I felt about you but also that I couldn't be here for a while after what I saw."

I reach for his hand, taking a deep breath. "I'm so sorry, Az. I was angry and hurt that I was a bastard child. I pushed you away. I wanted you to feel pain just like I was feeling." I look away. I feel ashamed of my immature behavior.

His finger touches my jaw, pushing my face back to his. He leans in slowly, never taking his eyes off mine. Our lips are so close, but not touching. He gently places his warm lips on mine as our surroundings fade away. Our movements are in sync, and I can feel the passion and love. I grab Az's shirt and fall back on the bed.

"I missed you," I moan into his mouth.

As we kiss, Az slides his tongue into my mouth, teasing me. My breath catches, and I fist the back of his shirt.

He pulls away, leaving me breathless. This is the first time we properly French kiss, and I liked it.

"We will not go further. It's time we talk." He sits up, pulling away from me.

Alrighty, then.

"First off, I want to let you know that was a magical kiss." He winks at me.

He pats the empty space beside him. I smile and slide over to him.

"I missed you. It hurt to leave you, but I needed to go back home to think. We are just teenagers, still trying to find our way in life," he says, eyes clouded with tears.

I start to fumble with my hands and look down at them. "I get it. I push everyone I love away. I'm broken." I look back up at him with a serious look. "I'm done running. I saw my mom at graduation. She told me to never doubt her love. Just hearing those words helped me heal my broken heart." I want to say more, but I don't.

"My yaya told me that all girls can act crazy sometimes, but a good-hearted one is a keeper. See, Emma, you are a generous, gracious, and compassionate young woman. We all struggle with life. You just lost your way for a little bit. I questioned everything about our relationship. I went through every scenario of how to move forward and for us to remain friends." He leans down and moves closer to my face, but not too close.

My heart is beating so fast and out of control. He's about to tell me that, even though he loves me, we can't be more than friends. I don't know if I can only be his friend.

I'm about to speak when his fingers lie against my lips.

"I don't want either one of us to screw this up. Starting college is going to be huge. Are you positive you want to start a relationship right now? Emma, you are it for me. In my culture, we love hard and we fight to keep what we have."

I reach out to wrap my hand around his neck, pulling him closer to me. "I love you, Az. You're it for me too. We are young, but love can conquer all. I'm all in." I crash my lips to his.

He smiles against my mouth. "I love you too, my crazy Emma."

We spend the next hour talking about his time

back home. I mention we should go to his hometown during one of our breaks from school so I can meet everyone. Plus, in the Philippines, the weather is warm.

EPILOGUE

Emma

One year later

"OHMYGOD, AZ! THAT feels so good," I cry out with pleasure.

"Emma, you're so stiff, and those knots need to be worked out," he barks while digging his thumbs into my shoulder blades. "I told you to stop carrying that heavy bookbag. I got you a roller one to help prevent this."

I didn't know your body could hold so much tension from a heavy bag. But to have his hands all over me like this makes it worth it.

I wiggle down in the cool sheets. His hands move down my back, making me arch up. I feel much better now, and my lady parts are getting excited.

Our first time was so romantic. He took me on a picnic to Jocassee park. One of his roommates let him borrow his parents' boat. After our lunch, he took me to the waterfall we found during our first time there. Behind the waterfall was a long rock slab.

We dove in the beautiful cold mountain lake, racing to the fall. He won, of course. I laughed when a fish nibbled on his toe and he started to scream. When I made it to the falls, I was breathless. I was not in shape for the long swim, but I would do anything for Az.

He helped me up onto the slick rock, wrapping his arms around me. The mist coming off the waterfall was chilly.

"You're so beautiful and you're mine," he said to me.

In that second, his lips came crashing down on mine. My body was on fire. The cold water that felt chilly just a moment ago was now cooling me off. I rubbed his back with my hands, following down till I got to his ass. I squeezed it. He moaned. He stepped back and separated our lips. I missed him right away. He walked over to a hole that sat far back in the corner and pulled out a towel. He unfolded it, laying it down on the rock.

"I came here earlier and hid it here. I want our first time to be special."

He swiftly picked me and led us farther back from the water. He slowly laid me down. He pressed soft kisses to my stomach then moved down. I ran my fingers through his hair. He continued down.

"Earth to Emma!" I feel a smack on my butt.

Dang, I must have fallen asleep.

"Only my princess would knock out during a sexy massage." He laughs, smacking my ass again.

"I was dreaming of our first time." I roll over and the sheet falls.

He leans down and kisses me forcefully. "Well, it's your lucky day. I'll show you, instead of letting you dream about it."

He pulls his shirt over his head then pulls his shorts and underwear off, quickly discarding my clothes as well. He presses his bare skin against mine, settling between my legs. He takes one of my legs and lifts it around him. He slowly slides inside me. I moan and lift, wanting more. He starts slow but then moves faster.

"Every time is better with you. I love you," he says and starts to thrust harder.

"Love you to the moon, Az." I come, and waves of pleasure take over my body.

I'm truly happy. We were both destined to be together. Our love is pure and one in a million to find. People say we will soon drift apart, but I know deep down that they are full of shit. If we both love each other, then we will fight to keep our love alive.

My cell phone rings.

"Shit, your dad has cameras in your apartment. He probably just saw us," Az says, rolling off me.

I reach for my phone. Beckham's name appears. I click to answer. "Sis, I need you. I'm in trouble. Go to the Trinity clubhouse at—"

Click. He hangs up.

I sit up and dial his number. It goes to voicemail. I reach down for my clothes and start putting them on.

"Beckham is in trouble. I've got to go find him. It's not like him to need me." I start to cry.

Az gets dressed. He refuses to let me go by myself. I don't know why Beckham would be at a biker clubhouse, but I will get my answer soon.

THE END

Made in the USA
Middletown, DE
10 May 2025